London Borough of Tower Hamlets

910000008097754

KT-494-571

Flappy
Entertains

Also by Santa Montefiore

Meet Me Under the Ombu Tree
The Butterfly Box
The Forget-Me-Not Sonata
The Swallow and the Hummingbird
The Last Voyage of the Valentina
The Gypsy Madonna
Sea of Lost Love
The French Gardener
The Italian Matchmaker
The Affair
The House by the Sea
The Summer House
Secrets of the Lighthouse
A Mother's Love
The Beekeeper's Daughter
The Temptation of Gracie
The Secret Hours
Here and Now

The Deverill Chronicles

Songs of Love and War
Daughters of Castle Deverill
The Last Secret of the Deverills

Santa Montefiore

Flappy Entertains

**SIMON &
SCHUSTER**

London · New York · Sydney · Toronto · New Delhi

First published in Great Britain by Simon & Schuster UK Ltd, 2021

Copyright © Santa Montefiore, 2021

The right of Santa Montefiore to be identified as author of
this work has been asserted in accordance with the
Copyright, Designs and Patents Act, 1988.

3 5 7 9 10 8 6 4 2

Simon & Schuster UK Ltd
1st Floor
222 Gray's Inn Road
London WC1X 8HB

Simon & Schuster Australia, Sydney
Simon & Schuster India, New Delhi

www.simonandschuster.co.uk
www.simonandschuster.com.au
www.simonandschuster.co.in

A CIP catalogue record for this book
is available from the British Library

Hardback ISBN: 978-1-3985-0033-4
Trade Paperback ISBN: 978-1-3985-0034-1
eBook ISBN: 978-1-3985-0035-8
eAudio ISBN: 978-1-3985-0195-9

This book is a work of fiction. Names, characters, places and incidents are either
a product of the author's imagination or are used fictitiously. Any resemblance
to actual people living or dead, events or locales is entirely coincidental.

Typeset in the UK by M Rules
Printed and bound in Great Britain by CPI Group (UK) Ltd, Croydon, CR0 4YY

*Dedicated to my dear friends
whose exceeding good humour has kept me sane
during Lockdown*

*Tiff Beilby
Lisa Carter
Brigitte Dowsett
Wendy Knatchbull
Clare Rutherford*

Chapter 1

Badley Compton, Devon, 2010

Flappy Scott-Booth, the self-styled queen of the small but not insignificant Devon town of Badley Compton, sat on the high-backed Russian imperial chair she'd bought at auction from Christie's and scrutinized the fresh face of the young woman sitting formally, and a little nervously, on the other side of the antique walnut desk. The girl was no beauty, but Flappy was not looking for that. She was looking for efficiency, capability, honesty and obedience. After all, she saw enough beauty every time she looked in the mirror, for, in her sixties, Flappy was undeniably still a strikingly good-looking woman. Her cheekbones were high, her chin strong, her aquamarine eyes set wide apart and framed by long, jet-black lashes. Her skin was flawless and her hair, dyed an ash-blonde colour, was cut into a precise bob that enhanced the sharp line of her jaw and ensured she stuck out in a crowd. Only her lips were on the thin side, revealing, in their tendency to turn down, a critical and unforgiving nature. No, she was not after a beauty; there was only room at Darnley for *one* of those.

'One is terribly busy, you see,' Flappy said in her slow, well-articulated voice. 'Of course, one really wants to be all things to all people, but that's simply not possible. Darnley is not just a home where I live with Mr Scott-Booth, it is the very heartbeat of Badley Compton. Being the biggest house in the town with endless gardens and lawns and,' she sighed, for such privilege came with a terrible weight of responsibility, 'an arboretum among other splendours too plenty to mention. Oh, we are so *so* lucky. But sometimes, it's just too much to take care of on one's own. You see, the diary is full of events. All year round we open our doors to the local community. For three weeks in June we share our gardens with the public so that they can enjoy this uniquely magical place. Then there's the garden party in July, the jumble sale in September, the Harvest Festival tea at the beginning of October and the Halloween children's fancy dress parade at the end, Bonfire Night in November, the Christmas dinner in December and then, of course, the weekly book club meetings, church meetings, parish meetings. I could go on.' She sighed again and fixed her piercing, aquiline eyes on the young woman listening attentively opposite her. 'But I won't. You will see for yourself how very busy one is and why one is in need of a Girl Friday. Someone to ease the load. You see, I did have a dear friend called Gracie, who used to be enormously helpful with all the arrangements, but then she went off to Italy last spring, met a count and married him. At sixty-eight, imagine! She's a countess now, which is lovely for her because she wasn't anything before. Just a very ordinary woman. I mean, you wouldn't have done a double take if you'd seen her in the street.' Flappy gave a little sniff and managed a tight smile. 'But I've been very understanding and generous because, I can tell you, it was extremely inconsiderate of her to leave me in the lurch like this. I need a personal assistant. You, Persephone, I believe, will be just the thing.' She lifted her interviewee's curriculum vitae off the desk. 'You have lots of experience. You speak Italian, French and Spanish, are a good organizer and you can cook, which is marvellous, even though I have a darling girl called Karen who does a teeny bit of cooking every now and then when things get too busy. I'm an excellent cook, of course, but one simply can't be everywhere all at once and my expertise is required in so many other places besides the kitchen.' She looked at her directly. 'Is there anything you *can't* do?'

'Garden?' Persephone replied uncertainly, hoping that the admission wouldn't cost her the job.

Flappy laughed and waved a manicured hand. 'Well, I can do without that. We are so *so* lucky to have an army of gardeners here at Darnley – and a sweet little Polish girl who comes to clean every morning, so I don't require you to do that either.' She put the CV back on the desk and tapped it with long talons, painted an elegant shell pink. 'I need you to start straight away.'

Persephone's eyes lit up with delight. 'Oh, that's wonderful. Thank you,' she gushed.

'I want you ready for work in the hall and looking

presentable at nine every morning. Hair tied back, shirt ironed, skirt below the knee, and tights. I cannot abide bare legs. And I don't like high heels.' Flappy screwed up her nose. 'Frightfully common. Now, is there anything you would like to ask me?'

'How would you like me to address you?' Persephone asked.

'Mrs Scott-Booth will do. Oh, and most importantly, when you answer the telephone I would like you to say, "Darnley Manor, Mrs Scott-Booth's assistant speaking." Is that understood?'

Persephone nodded. 'Absolutely,' she replied. 'Absolutely, Mrs Scott-Booth.'

Flappy smiled. This twenty-five-year-old was a quick learner.

After Persephone had gone, Flappy remained at her desk in her study and glanced out of the window. This charming room, decorated so tastefully in muted greens and greys, had a pleasing view of the garden. Well, of *one* of the gardens. Flappy was very fortunate at Darnley to have more than one. To have a whole array, in fact, to show off to her friends and the local community. This particular garden was called the croquet lawn, even though no one played croquet on it. They used to, of course, when her four children were young, but now they had flown the nest and gone to live in various faraway corners of the globe, the lawn was used for events. The ground was perfectly flat for a marquee and along the left-hand side ran an old stone wall, in front of which was planted the widely celebrated herbaceous border. Flappy was very proud of this feature and delighted in giving people the 'Darnley Manor Herbaceous Tour', which involved walking at a stately pace and pointing out the various plants, using their correct names, of course, which she had committed to memory. 'Subalpine larkspur' sounded much more exotic than the more common name 'delphinium', and 'hemerocallis' gave the day lily a certain mystique. Even a petunia was rendered more alluring when called by its botanical name *Ruellia brittoniana*. She had four full-time gardeners, dressed in green T-shirts and khaki trousers, who did all the hard work, but occasionally (and especially if she was expecting guests) Flappy herself would pick up her barely used pair of secateurs and waft around the rose garden, lopping off the odd dead head. Now she waved at one of the young lads who was pushing a wheelbarrow across the lawn. He tipped his hat. She smiled graciously, because Flappy was always gracious whatever her mood, then returned to the matter at hand. The questions she was going to raise at the Badley Compton ladies' book club meeting the following evening.

The telephone rang.

Flappy counted the rings, then answered on the eighth ring to give the impression that she was exceedingly busy and had perhaps had to walk a great distance to reach it. 'Darnley Manor, Flappy Scott-Booth speaking.'

'Flappy, I have news.'

It was Mabel. If Flappy was the self-appointed queen of Badley Compton, Mabel Hitchens was her eager-to-please lady-in-waiting. 'I hope I'm not interrupting you,' said Mabel breathlessly. 'I know how busy you are.'

'You know what they say, Mabel, give a job to a busy person and it will always get done. Busy people make time for everything. Now, what have you got for me?'

'Hedda Harvey-Smith has bought a house in Badley Compton,' said Mabel triumphantly, knowing almost without doubt that this would be news to Flappy, who liked to be the first to know everything.

There was a long pause as she digested this horrifying piece of information. Flappy had had the misfortune of meeting Hedda Harvey-Smith back in April when she had made an impromptu appearance at Hedda's brother's funeral. Back then, when Hedda had suggested she and her husband Charles were going to move to Badley Compton, Flappy had thought, indeed she had hoped, that it was just an idle threat. Now it seemed, if Mabel's source was to be believed, that the threat had been realized. She stiffened like a dog sensing a challenge to her territory and replied with well-practised breeziness, 'I'm not sure which house they will have bought, Mabel, as the only other big house in the town belongs to Sir Algernon and Lady Micklethwaite, and I don't imagine Hedda would deign to buy anything smaller than that.' She laughed, heartened by her logic. 'Are you sure you haven't got it wrong, Mabel?'

'*That's* the most intriguing thing about it, Flappy. The house Hedda has bought is indeed none other than Compton Court.' Mabel heard Flappy's sharp intake of breath and felt a frisson of satisfaction. This was *all* news to Flappy. 'The very one,' she continued, her voice rising with enthusiasm. 'Sir Algernon and Lady Micklethwaite have moved to Spain.'

If Flappy had not been sitting down already she would have sunk into her chair like a deflating soufflé. How was it possible that all this had happened right under her nose without her having the slightest notion of it? Surely Phyllida Micklethwaite should have informed her that they were leaving? Of course, Flappy couldn't count her as a friend, even though she had made many attempts over the years to acquire her as one, but it would not be wrong to consider her an acquaintance. Hadn't she attended many of Flappy's events, after all? In fact, she had been the guest of honour at her garden party back in July. Flappy sighed heavily and rallied. For if there was one thing Flappy was good at, it was hiding how flustered she really felt. 'I think it's wonderful that Hedda and Charles are coming to live here in Badley Compton,' she said, as gracious as ever. And then, all at once, a space cleared in Flappy's busy mind and a brilliant idea popped in. 'We must welcome them with a party,' she said. *Oh yes! A party, here at Darnley,* she thought to herself with a rush of excitement. *A lavish party to show Badley Compton that the queen feels no challenge to her position, and to let Hedda know early on that there is a hierarchy in this town and that she'd be best advised to adhere to it.* 'Do you know when they are moving in?' she asked.

'Ooooh! A party! How exciting, Flappy. No one throws a party like you!' When Flappy didn't reply, Mabel added quickly, 'John saw a big removal van heading that way this morning when he went out to buy the papers.' John was Mabel's husband. 'It was a very large and grand one. The kind of removal van a woman like Hedda Harvey-Smith would hire.'

'Indeed?' said Flappy ponderously.

'Oh yes. I bet it's full of treasures.'

'Yes, yes, I'm sure it is,' Flappy snapped, bristling at the thought of a very large and grand removal van full of Hedda Harvey-Smith's treasures. 'If they're moving in as we speak then we don't have much time. It will have to be in the next couple of weeks. The beginning of September. A cocktail party in the garden. The last of the summer parties. Something for everyone to look back on during the long winter months and talk about when it gets dark at three and is drizzling and cold. The garden still looks exquisite. In fact, Darnley has never looked more magnificent. I will telephone Hedda right away.'

'Oh, she'll be delighted to hear from you,' said Mabel innocently.

'Of course she will. If I welcome them warmly into the community, everyone else will follow my lead. And you know, Mabel, I'm very happy to give them a little leg-up. After all, it's nothing for me, is it? And it will mean so much to them.'

When Flappy put down the receiver her competitive spirit was already at boiling point. She flicked open her red leather address book and ran a polished nail down the index of gold letters until it landed on M. There, a few addresses beneath the mayor, were Sir Algernon and Lady Micklethwaite. She pursed her lips irritably at the thought of having to replace their address with the new one in Spain, thus making a mess of her immaculate book, but it couldn't be helped. She picked up the telephone and dialled.

After a great many rings a man's voice responded. 'Compton Court.'

'Ah, hello, to whom am I speaking? This is Mrs Scott-Booth of Darnley Manor,' said Flappy grandly.

'Good day to you, madam. I'm Johnson, the butler. I'm afraid the lady of the house is indisposed. Would you care to leave a message?'

Flappy was put out on two counts. One, because Hedda had a butler, and two, because the butler was clearly not aware of how important she was. 'Yes, if you would be so kind,' she said, digging deep to find her graciousness. 'Please will you let her know that Flappy Scott-Booth of Darnley Manor would like to welcome her into the community at a small gathering of like-minded people next week, here at Darnley. Nothing too elaborate, we country folk find ostentation frightfully vulgar. Perhaps she would be good enough to give me a call when she has a moment and let me know which day suits.' She promptly gave him her number.

'I will make sure she receives your message this morning,' said Johnson.

'That would be most kind, thank you.' Then she added, as an afterthought, 'If I'm not at home, my personal assistant Persephone will answer the phone and Mrs Harvey-Smith can leave a message with her.' Hedda might have a butler but *she* had a PA. Flappy put down the receiver, feeling very pleased with herself.

As usual, just before lunch, Kenneth Scott-Booth's caramel-coloured Jaguar purred into the forecourt of Darnley Manor and came to a smooth halt beside Flappy's shiny grey Range Rover. Kenneth opened the door and, with a groan because of the obstruction of his voluminous belly, he heaved himself off the seat and placed two pristine white golfing shoes firmly on the gravel. Barely five feet eight inches tall, in a pair of yellow tattersall plus fours, yellow socks and matching cashmere V-neck sweater, he might have cut a comical figure had he not been so seriously rich. Kenneth was not a man to be taken lightly. Nor did he take *himself* lightly. Here was a man who was reaping the rewards of seeds sewn shrewdly, playing regular rounds of golf on the course he had built in Badley Compton, which bore his name, and living life high on the hog. Golf, more than anything else, was what inspired him and propelled him through his days. After all, why should his hours be filled with anything less self-indulgent? Hedonism was his by right, for he had done his fair share of hard work building his empire of popular fast food restaurants in the 1970s, and selling it for millions ten years later. That had taken guile, cunning and good business acumen, which he had in abundance. He was a boy from the wrong side of the tracks who'd made good. And Flappy Booth, as she'd been called when he married her, was the cherry on his cake. It was she who had come up with the idea of joining their two names together. Thus, with the double-barrelled Scott-Booth, they gave themselves the one thing they lacked: an air of grandeur.

Kenneth flung open the front door and strode into the hall where two important-looking portraits of him and Flappy, by the famous artist Jonathan Yeo, were hung either side of the marble fireplace, and a chequerboard floor gleamed beneath exquisite eighteenth-century furniture. The hall was, indeed, very impressive at Darnley. He sighed with satisfaction. He could smell lunch. Was it lamb? He loved lamb. None of this vegetarian nonsense that Flappy had once flirted with. Kenneth was a man who liked his meat and two veg. 'Darling!' he called, standing squarely on the chequerboard floor with his hands on his hips.

Flappy emerged from her study and floated into the hall in a billowing pale blue shirt, white palazzo trousers and lots of gold jewellery. 'Darling,' she replied, offering him her cheek upon which he duly planted a kiss. 'Did you have a lovely morning?'

'Not bad. Not bad. I missed a short putt on the second. Should have bogeyed on the seventh – I usually do. If I hadn't hit my ball out of bounds on the eighteenth, I would have had one of my best rounds, ever.'

Flappy let his report go in one ear and out the other for she found golf a most tedious sport. It wasn't like tennis, which was glamorous. It was like darts, or pool, which were not. 'You must be starving, darling. Karen's cooked a leg of lamb. I told her to take it out of the Aga a little earlier this

11

time because we prefer it a teeny bit pink, don't we? I'm an expert at cooking lamb, as you know, but I've been so busy this morning I simply didn't have the time.'

He followed her upstairs, because Flappy knew he liked to change out of his golfing clothes before lunch. While he swapped the plus fours for chinos in his dressing room, Flappy sat at the vanity table in her bedroom next door and dabbed her pretty nose with a powder puff. It was exceedingly uplifting to look a good ten years younger than all the other women of her age in Badley Compton, she thought with a smile. 'I've taken on a PA,' she shouted. 'She's called Persephone and she's starting tomorrow.'

'Jolly good,' Kenneth shouted back. 'Six months in Olympus and six months in Hades,' he said with a chuckle.

'Oh and do you remember Hedda Harvey-Smith from Harry Pratt's funeral? The big woman with the loud voice.'

'There were lots of big women with loud voices,' he shouted back. 'Which one do you mean?'

'You know, darling. The one with lots of hair, brown, badly dyed, poor thing.' Flappy ran a hand down her expertly dyed ash-blonde bob. 'She considers herself very grand. You *know*, darling, Hedda Harvey-Smith.'

Kenneth didn't recall anyone by that name. 'Well, what about her?'

'She and her husband Charles have bought the Micklethwaites' house and are moving in today.'

There was a long pause. Then Kenneth appeared in her doorway, buttoning up his shirt. 'What's happened to the Micklethwaites?' he asked.

'They've gone to live in Spain.' Flappy shook her head and frowned. 'Didn't you know? I thought I'd mentioned it. Lady Micklethwaite told me herself some months ago. It must have slipped my mind.'

'Who did you say this woman was?'

'No one important.'

'Does she have a husband?'

'Apparently, he's called Charles.'

Kenneth nodded. 'I wonder if he plays golf.'

It wasn't until six o'clock that evening that Hedda Harvey-Smith called Flappy back. After the usual eight rings, Flappy picked up the phone. 'Darnley Manor, Flappy Scott-Booth speaking.'

'Ah, Flapsy. Hedda here,' said Hedda in a loud voice.

Flappy wasn't sure whether she'd misheard the pronunciation of her name. She assumed she must have, for everyone knew she was called Flappy, and carried on. 'Oh, Hedda,' she gushed, her voice saccharine. 'How good of you to call me back.'

'Been jolly busy with the move.'

'So I gather.' Flappy certainly wasn't going to let on that she'd only just found out. 'Welcome to Badley Compton.'

'Thank you, Flapsy. Delightful here. Charles and I couldn't be happier. Though it'll take more than a few days to get everything shipshape.'

Flappy was almost certain that Hedda had called her Flapsy again, but not certain enough to pick her up on it. However, the uncertainty unbalanced her. 'I know the Micklethwaites' house well,' she rallied. 'I can imagine just how much work you're having to do. Phyllida, Lady Micklethwaite, is a dear friend of mine, you know.'

'What can I do for you, Flapsy?'

'It's Flappy,' said Flappy firmly, now one hundred per cent certain she had heard correctly.

'What can I do for you, Flappy?' Hedda repeated, without missing a beat, or apologizing for getting it wrong.

Flappy took a deep breath, straining to find the charm and generosity of spirit for which she was so well known. 'I would like to welcome you and Charles with a little cocktail party here at Darnley,' she said, forcing her way through her irritation with a tight smile. 'It would be so nice to introduce you to the community. We in Badley Compton like to make newcomers feel at home.'

'That's awfully kind of you, Flappy,' said Hedda, not sounding nearly as grateful as Flappy hoped. 'But Charles and I are going to throw a little party of our own. You should receive your invitation tomorrow.'

Flappy didn't know what to say. She searched frantically for some way of restoring her position on the high ground, but could only come up with, 'How lovely, Hedda. So sweet of you. The community will be thrilled. They do love a good party.'

'I hope *you* can come,' said Hedda.

'I'll have a look in my diary. You know, one is so busy.'

'I do hope you can squeeze us in, Flappy,' Hedda replied. 'From what I hear a party wouldn't be complete without you.'

Flappy laughed, finding her place once more on the high ground and feeling secure again. 'Kenneth and I would love to come, I'm sure.'

Chapter 2

Flappy was an early riser. Kenneth was not. On top of that he snored, which was a consequence of drinking indecent amounts of red wine every evening, so Flappy had banished him to his bed in his dressing room, where he could grunt to his heart's content like a happy pig and lie in until nine. This banishment had started as a temporary measure so that Flappy could get her beauty sleep and dress in the morning without having to mind that she was disturbing her snoring husband. But the routine had set, as routines so quickly do, and it had now been eight years since Kenneth had slept in the marital bed. As for sex, Flappy considered it 'bestial' and was only too happy when, on turning fifty, she put an end to it once and for all. She announced to her husband that she would no longer be available for that kind of activity and he'd be well advised to put any excess energy into golf. This he did, with a great deal more passion than he had ever put into his wife.

By nine o'clock, when Persephone waited in the hall as requested, in a black pencil skirt that fell just below the knee, a crisp blue shirt, shiny brown hair tied into a ponytail and a notebook and pen at the ready, Flappy had already done an hour of yoga in the gym (which was located next to the indoor swimming pool), spoken to her daughter Mathilda, who lived with her husband and children in Sydney, and read the *Daily Mail* before anyone arrived to see that *that* was her newspaper of choice. She breezed into the hall in a pair of khaki cotton trousers, a tailored white shirt (inspired by Meryl Streep's Karen Blixen), elegant gold jewellery and smelling of Jo Malone's tuberose, and greeted her new PA with a smile. 'Ready for a very busy day?' she asked.

Persephone nodded. 'Absolutely, Mrs Scott-Booth.'

'Wonderful. Follow me.'

Flappy had set up a desk for Persephone in the library, a room which Kenneth never entered and Flappy only occasionally, to look something up or to show off to a visitor she wanted to impress, for impressive it was, the library at Darnley. Kenneth made no secret of the fact that he didn't read books, but he did manage to keep the secret that the rows and rows of beautifully glossy tomes had been bought en masse from a company that specialized in rich people's collections. Flappy, though never having opened a single one, claimed to be the intellectual in the family. 'If I don't have at least three books on the go, I feel bereft,' she would claim, before listing those she knew would impress.

Persephone placed her laptop on the desk, which was positioned in front of a wide window with a pretty view of a little garden enclosed by tall yew hedges (the Yew Garden), and waited for Flappy to give her her orders.

'Your first job is to make a list of five books I can recommend at tonight's book club meeting,' said Flappy.

'What genre of books, Mrs Scott-Booth? Biography, history, fiction? Light, heavy?' Persephone's pen was poised above her notebook and she had a very keen and expectant look on her face.

Flappy gave a supercilious sniff. 'Personally, I enjoy books by writers other people find a little heavy, like V.S. Naipaul and Salman Rushdie, two of my absolute favourites. But the ladies in the club prefer something a teeny bit lighter. It's meant to be fun and not too challenging. Although, personally, I believe it's imperative to challenge oneself, don't you, Persephone?'

'Yes, I do,' Persephone agreed. 'Would you like the list to be made up of contemporary authors or older ones?'

'Contemporary. I believe it's important to keep ahead of the curve, don't you?'

'I have some ideas already.'

'You do?' Flappy was pleasantly surprised.

'Yes, I'm a prolific reader like you, Mrs Scott-Booth. Although, I confess that, while I enjoyed *The Enchantress of Florence*, I find V.S. Naipaul too slow-paced for my taste.'

Flappy put her head on one side and gave her a sympathetic smile. 'Well, he's not for everyone.'

Kenneth appeared in the doorway, dressed in a green golfing ensemble. 'You must be Flappy's new PA,' he said, running his small eyes over her and grinning appreciatively. He liked girls in pencil skirts. It was a shame Flappy abhorred high heels.

Persephone put out her hand. 'It's very nice to meet you, Mr Scott-Booth.'

He shook it and glanced at his wife. 'Don't wear her out on her first morning, will you, eh?'

Flappy laughed. 'She might as well begin as she means to go on.'

She left Persephone in the library and followed her husband through the house and into the kitchen where *The Times* newspaper was waiting for him on the dining table. 'It's all yours, darling. I've read it,' she said breezily. 'The leader page is of particular interest.' He sat down and waited for Flappy to bring him his cup of coffee, which she did every morning, with her own cup of Earl Grey tea which she took with a slice of lemon (it was very common to drink it with milk). Then the two of them sat opposite each other to discuss the day's plans, as was their custom.

Just as Kenneth was glancing at his Rolex to see if it was time to leave for his game of golf, Persephone knocked tentatively on the kitchen door. 'Sorry to disturb you, Mrs Scott-Booth, but would you like me to open the post for you?' she asked, holding a pile of letters in her hand.

'That would be very kind, thank you.' Flappy's eyes dropped to the letters and narrowed. 'Is there a stiffy in there?'

'An invitation?' Persephone flicked through them and pulled out a big white envelope with 'Mrs Kenneth Scott-Booth' written in black calligraphy on the front.

'Yes, that's the one. I'll open it myself,' she said. Persephone handed it to her and left the room.

Flappy looked at it closely. The calligraphy irritated her at once. It was very classy. And the invitation itself was thick and stiff as tasteful invitations should be, which was also irritating. Even the wording was correct, not even a whiff of tackiness. Flappy gave a sniff and lifted her chin. 'It's from Hedda,' she told Kenneth. When he frowned, she elaborated. 'You know, the woman I was telling you about yesterday.'

'With the loud voice?'

'Yes, with the loud voice.' She sighed as if the very thought of Hedda's event was extremely tedious. 'She and Charles are throwing a cocktail party to introduce themselves to Badley Compton.'

Kenneth was thrilled. He loved a party. 'Good. When?'

'In a couple of weeks' time. At Compton Court.' Then, after a pause, 'I wonder who else they've invited.'

'Everyone,' said Kenneth.

'Well, not *everyone*, surely,' said Flappy disdainfully.

Kenneth got up and smiled down at his wife. 'Of course not everyone, darling. Only PLUs.' *Yes, people like us,* Flappy thought to herself with satisfaction. Anyone who took such trouble with their invitations would, of course, have been very selective.

Flappy longed for the telephone to ring so that Persephone could answer it, but she didn't have the time to wait around. So, she gave the girl a long list of things to do with regard to the jumble sale she was hosting in September and then left in her shiny grey Range Rover. As she drove into town in a pair of oversized sunglasses and trilby, she pondered the pros and cons of accepting Hedda's invitation. Were she to decline, she would have the satisfaction of being one up, for everyone would assume that she'd received a better invitation (and talk of nothing else but who that invitation could be from), but then she would have to hear the details of Hedda's party from Mabel, which would be very annoying. Besides, she was more than a little curious to see what Hedda's house looked like. If the truth be told, she had never set foot in the Micklethwaites' house.

Badley Compton was a pretty town of white houses with grey slate roofs built in the wide embrace of a cove. Behind it green hills undulated gently, cows grazed and sheep gambolled, and beneath it, in the calm water of the bay, fishing boats floated like ducks. Today, with the clouds resembling cotton-wool balls and the sun shining merrily in a bright blue sky, Badley Compton looked as charming as a postcard. Flappy parked her car outside Big Mary's Café Délice, which was the pulse of the town, and climbed out. She could see through the window of the café that it was busy.

She pushed open the door and was immediately accosted by the sweet smell of cakes. Big Mary Timpson was celebrated for her baking, but Flappy rarely allowed something so naughty to pass her lips. She didn't keep her elegantly slim figure by gorging on carbohydrates and sugar. 'Good morning,' she trilled, sweeping her eyes over the familiar faces in the café who all turned to look at her as she breezed in. Big Mary was in her usual place behind the counter, a red-and-white-striped apron stretched over her large bosom, her platinum-blonde hair falling in tight curls over her shoulders.

'Good morning, Mrs Scott-Booth,' she replied in a broad West Country brogue. 'What can I get you this morning?' Big Mary knew the answer even before Flappy had opened her mouth.

'Actually, I'm not here to make a purchase,' Flappy answered, glancing at the sticky buns and feeling sorry for all those weak-willed people who were unable to resist them. She approached the counter and lowered her voice. 'I'm here to talk about your . . . ' She hesitated. What exactly was Hedda to Big Mary? Then she remembered, for Flappy's internal filing system was unfailing. 'Your *aunt*, Hedda Harvey-Smith.'

Yes indeed, Hedda was the aunt who had appeared out of the blue. When loner Harry Pratt, who had lived a modest life in Badley Compton for sixty years, had died in April he revealed, in his will, that Big Mary Timpson was his illegitimate daughter (quite a surprise for Big Mary) and bequeathed her a great deal of money that no one knew he had. Then, to add to the shock, his sister, Hedda Harvey-Smith, who no one had ever heard of, turned up at his funeral and explained that money had meant nothing to Harry, who had sought a simple life living off memories of flying over the white cliffs of Dover in his Spitfire. Who'd have thought that Harry

Pratt was such a man of mystery? Flappy considered it 'admirable' that Big Mary continued to run her café as before, even though she apparently had enough money to retire on.

'Yes, she's just moved to Badley Compton,' said Big Mary.

'Indeed, and into such a beautiful house,' Flappy added. 'Phyllida, Lady Micklethwaite, was a dear friend of mine. Such a shame they decided to move to Spain.' She sighed with regret. 'Still, lovely for them to know that their beloved home will be inhabited by good people.'

'Nice for me too to have a relation just down the road,' said Big Mary. 'I thought I had no one and now I have Hedda and Charles. I consider myself very lucky.'

Flappy glanced around her to make sure she wasn't going to be overheard. 'I received my invitation today to their party,' she said in a voice so low that Big Mary had trouble hearing her.

'Good,' exclaimed Big Mary. 'It's going to be a great party.'

Flappy wished she'd keep her voice down; after all, it really wasn't kind to speak about it in front of people who weren't lucky enough to receive an invitation. 'I was going to throw a party myself, at Darnley, to welcome them into the community, but they got there first. Still, I'm sure Hedda was given good advice on whom to invite, and whom *not* to invite,' she added with a chuckle. 'One doesn't want to open one's door to any old nobody.'

Big Mary gave Flappy one of her most cheerful smiles. '*I* gave her the list,' she said.

'*You* did?' Flappy replied, hiding her surprise, for Flappy was a master at dissembling.

'Yes, Hedda didn't know where to begin.'

'Oh, how appropriate.'

'That's what she thought. After all, I know the people who loved Harry, and the nicest people from Badley Compton come into my café.'

'Quite,' Flappy agreed.

'So you don't need to whisper, because everyone in here has been sent an invitation.'

'Oh,' said Flappy again, feeling a little tight about the throat. 'How lovely. It really is a community affair then?'

'That's what Hedda wants.'

'Can I do anything to help?' Flappy asked, struggling to reassert herself. 'I have the most wonderful PA I could lend her.'

'Thank you very much for offering, Mrs Scott-Booth, but I think Hedda has everything under control.'

'I'm sure she has,' said Flappy. Her eyes strayed to the enticing display of cakes beneath the glass. 'On second thoughts, I'll buy a cake for Persephone, my PA.'

'That's a nice idea,' said Big Mary, taking down a pastel-pink box. 'Which one would you like?'

Flappy's mouth watered. 'The one with icing on it.'

'They're my favourites. I call them Devil's Desire.' Using a pair of tongs, Big Mary picked up the cake and placed it carefully in the box. 'I'll tell Hedda you popped in,' she said, handing Flappy the bag.

'Do,' said Flappy. 'And send her my best regards. I very much look forward to seeing her.'

Flappy climbed into the car and started the engine. So, Hedda had indeed invited everyone, she thought crossly. Had she asked Flappy, instead of Big Mary, she would have been given a far classier list of people to invite. Well, Hedda wasn't to know, of course, Flappy thought generously, because Flappy was, deep down, a very generous woman. But she would, in time. Flappy would make sure of it.

She lifted the pastel-pink box off the passenger seat and put it on her lap. Then she delved inside and took out the cake. A couple of minutes later it was gone.

That evening Flappy sat on the terrace in a floral sundress that reached her slim ankles, with a pale cashmere shawl thrown about her shoulders. She looked elegant and serene as she watched the shadows lengthen over the immaculately mown lawn and the birds flying into the trees to roost. When the doorbell went, she didn't get up as she normally would. She didn't have to. She'd asked Persephone to answer it for her and to show the ladies of the Badley Compton book club to the terrace, where Flappy was waiting for them with crystal flutes and an expensive bottle of prosecco on ice.

The first to arrive was Mabel Hitchens. She always made sure she was the first by turning up five minutes early. No one else would dare show themselves at Darnley Manor a moment prior to Flappy's invitation, but Mabel considered herself to be Flappy's closest friend, which gave her special status. The relationship, however, was not an equal one. Mabel admired Flappy and copied her style, although with her thin brown hair and ordinary looks such flair was beyond her capability. Flappy did *not* admire Mabel and thought she had no style at all, but she was quite fond of her. After all, a queen must always be surrounded by ladies who are both lesser and deferential. It does not do to be challenged.

Mabel followed Persephone through the house to the terrace, even though she had been coming to Darnley for thirty years. When she saw Flappy, she took in the pale chicness of her clothes and made a mental note to adorn herself in the same muted colours the next time she had to dress up. One always dressed up for Flappy, even though the invitations specifically stated 'informal'. In Flappy's world, there was no such thing. Standards must be upheld whatever the occasion, she maintained. As soon as one allowed them to slip one became as ordinary as the hoi polloi, which was Flappy's greatest fear.

'Hello, Flappy,' Mabel trilled, marvelling at the splendour of her host through thick spectacles, which made her watery grey eyes look large and starey. 'You look gorgeous. Like a painting. Yes, you look *just* like a painting. A beautiful work of art.'

'Oh really, this old dress? I just threw it on, without a thought. Grabbed the first thing I could find in my wardrobe,' Flappy responded in delight.

'I imagine everything in your wardrobe is gorgeous,' said Mabel, envisaging Flappy's wardrobe with envy.

'Have a glass of prosecco.'

'How lovely.'

'*Bellissimo*,' said Flappy. There was no point in knowing how to speak languages if one never used them. 'Isn't this *divertente*?'

26

'Oh yes, Flappy, very!' Mabel agreed as always, impressed by Flappy's knowledge of Italian.

'Now, I received a charming invitation this morning,' Flappy told her. 'Did you get yours?'

'From Hedda Harvey-Smith? Yes, I did. Isn't it exciting!'

'The whole town has been invited,' Flappy informed her. 'Isn't that generous of her, to invite everyone?'

'Oh yes, very generous,' Mabel agreed.

'You see, she asked Big Mary, who as you know is her niece, to put the list together for her. I mean, if I were her, I would have been a bit more discerning, but ... ' Flappy gave a sniff. 'She wouldn't have thought of calling *me* for advice, would she? After all, she barely knows me. Big Mary was all she had, which is a pity. Still, it will be great fun, I'm sure.'

'Perhaps, in future, when she knows you a little better, she'll draw on your wisdom in these matters. But if *you're* there, Flappy, it'll be great fun.'

The next to arrive were Sally Hancock, a brash woman with red hair and a penchant for glittery sweaters, and Esther Tennant, who couldn't care less about her hair or clothes because she spent most of her time on a horse. 'We're not late, are we?' said Sally, stepping onto the York stone in high heels.

'You're perfectly on time,' said Flappy, glancing at the inappropriate shoes with disdain. She picked up the bottle of prosecco and poured two more glasses.

'How lovely!' Sally gushed. 'This is just what I need after a whole day at my desk.' Sally wrote unashamedly trashy romances under the pseudonym Charity Chance.

'How's the new novel coming along?' Flappy asked, crinkling her nose to convey that, while she wouldn't dream of reading such a thing herself, she could appreciate the vast number of Charity Chance's readers. After all, someone had to entertain the uneducated masses.

'I'm about halfway through,' Sally replied, sinking into the fat cushions on the teak bench and taking a sip of prosecco.

'I don't know how you do it,' said Flappy. 'Such an imagination.'

Esther glanced at Mabel and the two women looked a little uneasy. Neither wanted to admit that they devoured Charity Chance.

'Sorry I'm late,' said Madge Armitage, scurrying onto the terrace in a tie-dye kaftan, her small feet clad in bejewelled flip-flops and her greying hair falling about her narrow shoulders in unbrushed tendrils. Flappy poured her a *small* glass of prosecco.

'Don't drink it all at once,' she said with a smile, but she wasn't joking.

Madge sat beside Esther and took a small sip because Flappy's sharp eyes were still upon her.

Flappy lifted her leather-bound notebook off the table and put on her reading glasses. 'Now, as we're all here, I've put together a list of books for you to choose from for our next meeting. I've thought very hard about each one. As you know, I do try to please you all, which is quite a challenge. But I think I've got it just right. The first one . . . '

'Did you all receive an invitation to Hedda Harvey-Smith's party?' asked Madge, who had downed the prosecco the moment Flappy's attention was diverted and was suddenly feeling rather brave. Flappy looked at her over her spectacles, but in spite of the scary expression on her face, Madge continued. 'Only, I've been dying to know, because I've never met Hedda Harvey-Smith so it was a lovely surprise to be invited.'

Flappy took off her glasses. 'Everyone has been invited,' she said in a bored tone of voice.

'Brilliant!' Esther exclaimed.

'Apparently the house is enormous,' Sally added.

'I suppose it has to be if she's invited everyone,' said Madge.

They all turned to Flappy. 'You *are* going to go, aren't you, Flappy?' Mabel asked.

Flappy inhaled through dilated nostrils and gave a small, secretive smile. 'I haven't yet decided,' she said. 'I confess, I have another invitation which I'm considering.'

Mabel gazed at Flappy in awe. It didn't surprise her one bit that Flappy had been invited elsewhere. 'What are you going to do? How can you choose?' she exclaimed. 'Only *you* could be so in demand, Flappy.'

'I'm going to struggle,' Flappy replied, pulling a face to show how hard that struggle was going to be. 'Truly I am. I don't want to let dear Hedda down and yet, the other invitation is very tempting.'

'What is it?' Esther asked.

'My lips are sealed,' said Flappy, pursing them.

'Ah, it must be something very important,' said Mabel.

'I'm afraid I cannot say.' Flappy smiled enigmatically.

'I do hope you choose Hedda's,' Mabel sighed. 'A party's not a party without *you*.'

Chapter 3

On Sunday morning Flappy was in a hurry to get to church. Kenneth, who liked to take his time over breakfast and read the Sunday papers in a leisurely fashion, was not. 'Why are you so desperate to get there on time?' he asked as she climbed into the passenger seat of his Jaguar fifteen minutes before the service was due to start. Normally they would be the last to arrive at one minute to ten. Everyone knew that.

'Because, darling,' she began as he climbed into the driver's seat and stretched the belt over his big belly. 'Our places in the front pew are not official, which means, when Hedda and Charles arrive, they might very well sit in them. There is nothing and no one to tell them they can't. But if *we* are in them they will understand the unspoken rule and not attempt to usurp them.'

Kenneth started the engine and the Jaguar purred contentedly. 'Why do you think they want to sit in the front row?'

'Because they have bought the biggest house in town. I suppose it *is* a teeny bit bigger than ours.'

'They might want to sit in the middle, or at the back. They might not be as competitive as you think they are.'

Flappy smiled patiently, as if she were explaining something very simple to a very simple person. 'Darling, you couldn't even remember who Hedda Harvey-Smith was, let alone what kind of woman she is. I can tell you, from the brief moments I have spent with her, that she is an exceedingly competitive woman.' She laughed lightly and gave a little sniff. 'Of course, she has no idea how transparent she is. How easy she is to read. I've always maintained that competitive people are just insecure people and should have our sympathy, not our condemnation. Still, it doesn't mean I'm going to allow her to sit in our seats in church. One's generosity has limits, doesn't it, Kenneth.'

'It does,' he agreed, because life ran more smoothly when he agreed with his wife.

'That is why we must get there early. Not too early, just five or so minutes. I'm sure Hedda will swan in at the last moment. I know her type. She will want to make an entrance.'

As Kenneth drew up and parked on the kerb, Flappy saw, to her dismay, a black Bentley already parked right in front of the gate that opened into the churchyard. She had never seen that car before, which meant only one thing: that it belonged to the Harvey-Smiths. Her skin bristled with rivalry. If it did, indeed, belong to Hedda and Charles, there could be no doubt that they were already inside the church, possibly at this very moment, lowering themselves into her and Kenneth's seats. An image of Hedda's large behind gave Flappy a moment's relief, because hers was small and toned due to her morning yoga sessions, but she was in too much of a hurry to savour her sense of superiority, she needed to get into church right away while there was still time to make an intervention.

Leaving Kenneth to catch her up she strode purposefully along the path. 'Did you see that Bentley?' she said to him when he reached her.

'A beauty,' he replied.

'I wouldn't trade my Range Rover for a Bentley, even if you paid me,' she said, lifting her chin. 'But then I'm terribly discreet. I'm not sure discretion is one of Hedda Harvey-Smith's most notable qualities.'

They entered the church to find the pews packed and the congregation full of chatter. Flappy's aquiline vision immediately honed in on Hedda Harvey-Smith at the front of the church, talking to the vicar. Without a moment's hesitation, Flappy marched down the aisle. She didn't look to her left or right, or acknowledge the expectant faces of her friends who turned to her like sunflowers. She didn't have time to bestow greeting. Right now she had an important matter to attend to.

As she approached them, the vicar raised his eyes and smiled at her, for besides being the local vicar, he was also a friend. After all, it was important for the queen of Badley Compton to be on good terms with God.

Hedda, noticing his straying gaze, turned round. When she saw Flappy, her expression changed. She beamed a smile, the kind of smile one gives to a cherished old friend one hasn't seen in a very long time. 'Flappy, my dear,' she said, holding out her hands.

Flappy returned her smile, although it didn't quite reach her eyes, and took the sturdy, unmanicured hands. 'Hedda, how lovely to see you.'

'You look so well, Flappy. Have you been away?'

'We always spend a couple of weeks in our house in the Algarve in July. I suppose I have retained my tan, although I never *ever* put my face in the sun.'

'That's why you look so young,' said Hedda. Then, to Flappy's astonishment, she sat down in Flappy's seat. Without apology or hesitation, or the slightest indication that she was even aware of the faux pas she was making, she plonked herself down as if it were just an ordinary pew. A moment later, before Flappy had time to prevent it, a breathtakingly handsome, grey-haired man, who Flappy realized with a stab of envy was Hedda's husband Charles, came and sat beside her, in Kenneth's seat. Flappy, for once in her life, was dumbfounded. She stood there, lips parted in amazement, eyes wide with horror.

'Ah, Flappy, there you are,' said Kenneth, rescuing her in the nick of time. 'Why don't we sit on the other side in the third pew. There are two free places.'

Flappy was not to be defeated. She inhaled through her nostrils, gathered her wits and smiled graciously down at Hedda and Charles. For if there was one thing Flappy was good at, it was being gracious in times of crisis. 'Hedda darling, you and Charles are in our seats.' She put out her hand to prevent them from getting up. 'Please, no apology. I'm delighted that you enjoy the view from the front row. We've enjoyed it for over twenty years, it's the least we can do to share it with you, who have just arrived in Badley Compton.' She shifted her eyes to Charles, who was gazing at her with the most beautiful green eyes she had ever seen. They were the colour of sea glass and as mesmerizing as Kipling's Kaa. Flappy caught her breath, falling suddenly into the beautiful green.

'Flappy Scott-Booth,' he said in a voice so aristocratic it seemed to vibrate over her body in a delightful caress.

'Yes,' she breathed.

'It's a pleasure to meet you. I've heard so much about you.'

'Oh,' said Flappy, forgetting suddenly how to speak.

'You're as charming as they say you are,' he said, and then he smiled and Flappy's stomach flipped. It had never done that before, not even when Kenneth had flashed the Cartier diamond engagement ring at her on the terrace of the Palace Hotel in St Moritz. With her legs turned to dough and the words still lost in muddled thought, she dug deep, very deep, for her willpower and managed to tear herself away.

Flappy, in the third row, which was a terrible affront to her dignity, was unable to keep her eyes on the vicar. She could only see the back of Charles's head and a sliver of his profile, but it was enough. How on earth had Hedda managed to ensnare such an attractive man? Of course, she wasn't *un*attractive herself, her face was pleasant enough and her eyes, big and brown, were warm and intelligent, but if one judged them from the perspective of the food chain, she and

Charles were on very different levels. He was a white tiger or a silver fox, and Hedda was – Flappy narrowed her eyes and considered Hedda's stout body, her thick brown hair and long eyelashes – an Ayrshire cow, she concluded with satisfaction.

The vicar gave a rousing sermon, to which Flappy would have normally listened with great focus so that she could comment on it later, but today she didn't hear a word, not a syllable. Her mind was whirring and not with the things with which it usually whirred. Never before in her life had she been so immediately smitten. Never before had she felt so powerless to resist. Never, not ever, had she felt 'bestial' without, at the same time, feeling utterly embarrassed and ashamed. Charles Harvey-Smith, in a few short sentences and one very long, lingering look, had awakened the beast within and Flappy was a new woman.

At the end of the service Flappy and Kenneth made their way out into the sunshine. They shook hands with the vicar, who stood at the big double doors beside a pair of children holding silver collection plates, and thanked his congregation for coming. 'How Christian of you to give the Harvey-Smiths your seats,' he said with a grateful smile, which would normally have given Flappy a frisson of pious delight, but she was so distracted by Charles she barely heard him.

'They're not *our* seats,' said Kenneth, giving his hand a firm shake then dropping a fifty-pound note into the collection plate.

'Unofficially, they are, Kenneth,' the vicar replied, taking back his hand with a wince. 'It was kind of you to give them up.'

'We don't mind where we sit, do we, Kenneth?' said Flappy, aware that Charles and Hedda were just behind them in the queue to greet the vicar and might easily overhear. 'As long as we can enjoy your rousing sermon, Graham, we're very happy anywhere.'

Flappy moved into the churchyard and was immediately accosted by Mabel. 'Did you see Hedda's husband, Flappy?' she hissed, barely able to contain her excitement.

'Her husband, why, what about him?' said Flappy coolly.

'He's so handsome!' Mabel could barely contain herself.

'Oh, do you think so?'

'Don't you?'

'I hadn't noticed.'

'You hadn't?'

'Not really. I thought he was charming, but as for his looks, well, you know me. I like to see beyond the superficial. A person's looks can be very misleading, and character is so much more important.'

'I'm sure you're right, Flappy. Ah, there he is now, coming out of the church.'

Flappy turned to look at this Adonis, a head taller than everyone else, grey hair silver in the sunshine, now making his way slowly towards her with his stout wife by his side. Flappy smiled and said to Mabel in a low voice, 'Indeed, he's very nice-looking. How clever of you to spot that, Mabel.'

Flappy's eyes twinkled at him flirtatiously. She was aware of her beauty and hadn't forgotten how to use it.

'Thank you very much, Flappy, for giving up your seats,' he said, his gaze penetrating right into her and giving her feelings she hadn't had in decades, or perhaps ever. 'Had we known, we would have sat elsewhere.'

Flappy waved her hand as if it was but a trifle. 'Oh, think nothing of it. Really, I'm delighted you sat there,' she said, giving him her most charming smile.

'You're very kind,' Hedda added. They both looked at Mabel.

'May I introduce you to Mabel Hitchens,' said Flappy, watching Mabel's delight as she shook hands with Charles.

'I'm very excited about your party,' Mabel gushed. 'You're so generous to invite everybody.'

Hedda smiled. 'The idea is to meet as many people in Badley Compton as possible and to make lots of new friends. It's thrilling starting again in a new place. We were so tired of London and the relentless social scene. I imagine it'll be a little sleepier down here, which will be a blessing.'

'Are *you* coming?' Charles asked Flappy and Flappy could tell from those deep green eyes that he really wanted her to.

'Flappy has another invitation, don't you, Flappy?' said Mabel, pulling a sad face. 'Such a shame. A party's not a party without Flappy!'

'Oh,' said Charles, looking disappointed. 'That *is* a shame.'

'Yes, it is,' agreed Hedda, looking even more disappointed.

'I *am* coming,' Flappy said at last. 'I declined the other invitation only this morning. I wouldn't miss your party for the world.'

Mabel clapped her hands. 'That's wonderful news, Flappy.'

'I *am* glad,' said Hedda. 'I imagine it'll be a year before we throw another one.'

'What fun! An *annual* party,' gushed Mabel. 'The last party of the summer. What a way to end it!'

Flappy would have been annoyed had it not been for Charles, whose gaze was warming her up on the inside like the first gulp of a margarita. 'Do you play golf?' she asked him.

When Kenneth came to take his wife home, she was still talking to Hedda and Charles. 'Ah, darling, come and meet my new friends,' Flappy said happily. 'Charles plays golf. Isn't that fun!'

Kenneth was very keen to meet a fellow golfer and gave his hand a vigorous shake. Unlike the vicar, Charles didn't flinch but returned the shake with equal vigour. The two men smiled at each other in the way fellow golfing men do. 'Flappy finds golf dull and my golfing friends even duller,' Kenneth told Charles with a playful roll of the eyes.

'Oh, you do exaggerate, darling!' Flappy replied. 'I was thinking, actually, of taking it up myself. I was rather sporty in my day, even though my long legs were often more of a hindrance than a help.'

'Hedda's a terrific golfer,' said Charles.

'Really?' Flappy replied incredulously. Hedda looked like she lay on a sofa all day eating marshmallows.

Hedda patted Flappy's arm with a bejewelled hand and winked. 'I'll give you a lesson or two, if you like, Flappy,' she suggested and all Flappy could do was smile back and reply:

'I can't think of anything I'd like more.'

As soon as Flappy arrived home she hurried upstairs to her bedroom to change. She always changed out of her church attire into something more comfortable and less formal. As it was a warm day she chose a pair of wide, sky-blue slacks and a crisp white shirt, which she wore loose and accessorized with a blue scarf and big gold earrings. Liking herself very much in the mirror, she went to the window and gazed out over the lawn, but she didn't notice the tidy stripes where it had been mown or the beauty of the sunlight that caught the leaves and made the trees shimmer because all she saw was Charles Harvey-Smith, gazing down at her with those hypnotic green eyes. Once again she considered Hedda and how extraordinary it was that a woman like her had managed to catch a man like him. It was extraordinary, she told herself. Just extraordinary.

But he had looked at *her*. A deep, probing and *predatory* look. The kind of look a man does not give his wife. She shivered with desire. She put a hand to her throat and took a deep breath. It was imperative that she control herself, she thought firmly as the shiver intensified, reaching parts of her she hadn't considered in decades. She was a woman in her sixties, she reminded herself – albeit a very beautiful woman with an impossibly slender and firm body – not a young woman in the first throes of love. She was also married. So was Charles.

Oh, but what fun to have a flirtation!

Flappy went and sat on the edge of her bed. On the little table, beneath the pile of novels by V.S. Naipaul and Salman Rushdie, none of which had ever been opened, lay the latest and very dog-eared novel by Charity Chance, entitled *Rite of Passion*. She pulled it out and looked at the cover, which was a photograph of a beautiful woman in a clinch with a ridiculously handsome and shirtless Latin man. She imagined herself in a similar clinch with Charles, but preferably with his shirt on. It was too early in the infatuation to undress him, she thought. There was no harm in that, was there? It was a daydream, that was all. Kenneth would never know. No one would. It would be her little secret. She settled back against the cushions and put on her reading glasses. She had a couple of hours to kill before lunch, so what better way to spend them than to indulge in a little erotica.

Chapter 4

Flappy knew what she had to do. She had thought about it all night and now, in the bright light of dawn as she held her Downward Dog, stretching out her calves and the backs of her thighs, she was in no doubt about the course she had to take. It was the only way. Sacrifices had to be made, but they would be worth it. She *had* to see Charles again, and soon. The only way to do that was to befriend Hedda. To make her not just a friend, but a *best* friend. She would start today. There was no better time than the present, after all.

During breakfast with Kenneth she carried out Stage One of her plan. 'Darling, why don't you ask Charles Harvey-Smith to play golf with you?' she suggested. 'It would be a nice thing to do, considering they've just moved down here and know no one.'

Kenneth looked at his wife with admiration. 'You are always thinking of other people, Flappy. That's what I admire about you most. Your generosity of spirit. I don't know anyone who would be as thoughtful as you.'

'Well, it would be very easy to sit here in our beautiful

house, with our beautiful gardens and our beautiful life, and think only about myself. But I cannot. I just cannot. Poor Hedda and Charles have left their home in London and all their friends and come down here to start again. It's the least I can do to include them and make them feel welcome.'

'I will call him this morning.'

'Do. He'll be so pleased. I'm going to invite them for dinner.' (That was Stage Two.)

'That's a good idea,' said Kenneth.

'I'll invite Graham and his charming wife, Joan. Make it a supper for six. Just an informal little kitchen supper, nothing special. I'll see if I can find that delightful young man who plays the harp and get him to give us a recital after dinner. That would be nice, wouldn't it?' Flappy sighed. 'I've set the bar rather high recently with my after-dinner entertainments, it's going to be exhausting finding something to better them. But better them I will, because I'd like Hedda and Charles to see how things are done here at Darnley. We might not be as cosmopolitan as London, but we do appreciate culture and refinement. Everyone says how special our dinner parties are, we cannot disappoint, can we?'

Kenneth put his hand on his wife's. 'Don't overdo it now, darling. I know how you enjoy giving people something special, but it's a lot of work and you already have too much on your plate. There's nothing wrong with a simple dinner, is there?'

'Of course not. If I can't find the harpist, or that delightful ex ballet dancer from the Royal Ballet who performed the

Dying Swan so beautifully, I will leave it. After all, when it comes to conversation, no one does it better than me.'

Persephone was waiting in the hall at nine. Flappy greeted her cheerfully and Persephone noticed how her cheeks were flushed this morning, as if she'd been on a run, and her eyes were very clear and sparkling. Flappy looked exceedingly well. 'Come with me, Persephone. I have lots for you to do today,' said Flappy, setting off across the hall. Once in the library, Flappy gave her Hedda's number. 'Get her on the line for me, will you?' she said.

Dutifully, Persephone dialled and waited. After a few rings, Johnson's voice answered. 'Hello, my name is Persephone Finley. I'm calling on behalf of Mrs Scott-Booth of Darnley Manor for Mrs Harvey-Smith. Might she be available to speak?' Flappy smiled her approval and Persephone nodded. She put her hand over the receiver and whispered, 'He's going to have a look.' A moment later she held out the telephone. 'Mrs Harvey-Smith is on the line.'

'Hedda,' said Flappy, perching on the edge of the desk and crossing her legs. 'Good morning.'

'Flappy,' said Hedda. 'How lovely to hear you. I was just going around the house with the builder. There's still so much to be done and I want it all finished before our party.'

'I'm sure there is. A big house like yours. Are you doing a great deal?'

'Purely cosmetic. Nothing structural. We're lucky that the bones of the house are so lovely, we didn't have to knock

43

down any walls like we had to do in London. Really, that was a terrible headache. This is a pleasure. I'm enjoying nesting. Like a contented hen. What can I do for you?'

'I'd love to invite you and Charles for supper. Nothing formal, just us and the vicar and his wife, who are dear, dear friends. I'm sure you'd like to meet the vicar properly, after all, he presided over the funeral of your darling brother Harry. It was a beautiful service, wasn't it?'

'We'd love to come,' said Hedda enthusiastically. 'I remember your garden and how lovely it was in April. I bet it's even lovelier now, in August.'

'Everything's gone a bit wild,' said Flappy, sighing mournfully. 'You know how it is at the end of the summer. The best is over, but it's still looking gorgeous. We're so *so* lucky to have such beautiful gardens at Darnley. Which day would suit you and I'll ask the vicar.'

'Shall we say Thursday?' Hedda suggested. 'Everyone's being very kind, we're out every evening this week but Thursday.'

'People are very welcoming here in Badley Compton,' said Flappy, wondering where they were going and who they were going with. She'd had an image in her mind of the two of them eating dinner alone in their fine dining room, surrounded by boxes yet to be unpacked, wondering whether they'd perhaps been a little rash in leaving London for Badley Compton. She was wrong. Hedda and Charles were in such demand she was lucky to have booked them in at all.

'Charles is heading off to the golf course now to meet Kenneth,' said Hedda. 'I gather it's named after you.'

'Named after Kenneth,' said Flappy. 'He built it.'

'How generous of him to give such a wonderful gift to Badley Compton.'

'It suits him too, Hedda. He's obsessed with golf.'

Hedda laughed. 'Charles got into it when he retired. Though, it hasn't yet turned into an obsession. Personally, I prefer bridge. Do you play bridge, Flappy?'

'I adore bridge,' said Flappy.

'Good. I'm looking for a fourth. Would you like to play this evening?'

'This evening? Oh, I'm not sure ...' Flappy didn't want to look as if she had no plans.

'I've got two ladies but I'm in need of one more to make the four.'

'Well, I suppose if you *need* me,' said Flappy slowly, in a tone of voice that suggested she would reluctantly cancel the plans she had already made for this evening to be of help to Hedda. 'I'm sure I can free myself up.'

'Wonderful,' said Hedda, with a distinct lack of gratitude, Flappy noticed. 'Six o'clock here at Compton Court.'

When Kenneth returned home for lunch, Flappy was just winding up the meeting for the jumble sale event in September. She was in the drawing room with the five ladies of the committee and Persephone, who was now closing her notebook and putting away her pen. The ladies were perched on the edge of the cream-coloured sofas, barely daring to lean back against the neatly arranged pointy cushions behind them for fear of disturbing the immaculate room. It was indeed immaculate, the drawing room at Darnley. The air smelt of the expensive scented candles Flappy always lit when she had guests and on the mantelpiece, in front of a vast gilt-framed mirror, was a glass vase of scented lilies. Flappy, in pale linen, sat comfortably in an armchair, bathed in a beam of sunlight that shone through the window behind her like a spotlight on a stage. She looked at each woman in turn, fixing them with her sharp eagle eyes, then said, in a slow and deliberate voice, 'Now, you all know what you're required to do, don't you? I'm afraid I must leave you to get on with it and trust that it will be done. I have a hectic afternoon ahead of me, so I must push on. If you have any questions, call Persephone.' Flappy smiled at Persephone. 'She's only just started working for me and I'm afraid I've thrown her into the deep end, haven't I, Persephone? But she's very capable. I'm so *so* lucky to have her.'

When the women had left and Persephone had gone to eat her sandwich in the garden, sitting on one of the many benches positioned in spots of great beauty for the public when they came in June, Flappy and Kenneth sat at the kitchen table to have the salad, new potatoes and cold ham that Karen had prepared for them. 'How was your golf?' Flappy asked.

'A very good day,' Kenneth replied.

'Do tell.' Flappy leaned across the table.

'Well ...'

'I'm longing to hear.'

'Well ...'

'From the beginning, darling. I'm all ears.'

'Well, Charles and I both had good approaches onto the green.'

'That's good,' said Flappy enthusiastically, looking at him steadily and giving him her full attention.

'On the final hole, he was four feet from the pin and I was a good ten feet. Don't want to brag, but I lined it up very carefully and it just dropped in. Very satisfactory. He was only four feet away, but it went round and round the edge of the hole and jumped out.'

'Did it!' Flappy exclaimed, laughing heartily. 'How clever you are, darling! Is Charles a good player?' She averted her eyes at this point in case Kenneth noticed the unusual flicker of interest in them. Flappy had never been interested in hearing about golf before and even less about his golfing friends. But Kenneth was only too happy to tell her about his morning. In fact, it gladdened him that she was, for once, taking an interest in something that mattered so much to him.

'He's a seven handicap,' Kenneth told her. 'But I don't think he was on his top form today.'

'But you were, weren't you, on top form?'

'Yes, I think I was.'

Flappy poured herself another glass of sparkling water and dropped in a slice of lemon. 'What's he like, Kenneth? Is he our sort of person, do you think?'

Kenneth shovelled a heap of lettuce leaves into his mouth. 'He's a good man,' he said.

Flappy smiled patiently. 'A *good* man.'

Kenneth nodded.

'What did he do? How did he make his money?'

Kenneth shrugged. 'I didn't ask him.'

'You didn't ask him?'

'We talked about golf.'

'What? All the way round the course?'

Kenneth nodded again. 'I'd say so.'

'I suspect he's exceedingly clever, don't you, Kenneth? He has a clever face, don't you think? An alive face. I have little time for dead faces, as you know. What one wants is a face full of character. The face of someone whose life is full and busy. I think Charles has that sort of face, don't you?'

Kenneth helped himself to more potatoes. 'These are delicious,' he gushed. 'What's she put on them?'

'Olive oil,' Flappy replied, knowing she'd get nothing more out of him. 'And salt.'

Flappy spent much of the afternoon working out what to wear for bridge. She didn't want to look like she'd tried too hard and yet she wanted to look elegant. Effortlessly elegant. She wasn't sure who was going to be there, of course, but she knew she'd know them. After all, she knew everyone in Badley Compton. She was quite excited to see Hedda's house, she had to admit, although she couldn't help being envious in anticipation. She envisaged the important-looking removal van full of treasures that Mabel had talked about and felt, in the middle of her chest, the familiar tightening of competitiveness. She *hated* competitive people. Hedda, she believed, was more competitive than most. Still, she needed

Flappy to make up her four at the bridge table. What sort of woman would Flappy be if she refused simply because she found Hedda a little competitive? If Flappy was good at one thing it was at rising above the likes of Hedda Harvey-Smith and not letting them get to her. She was a bigger beast. A white tigress to Hedda's Ayrshire cow.

Of course, there was a strong chance she would see Charles. She imagined those sea-green eyes smiling down at her and felt a lot better about the evening ahead. Hedda was a nice woman, in spite of her faults, and Flappy was very good at bridge; she was bound to have a nice time. And so it was, at ten to six, that Flappy climbed into her shiny grey Range Rover, dressed in a pair of white naval-style trousers and Breton striped sweater adorned with a large gold chain about her neck and gold bangles jangling on her wrist. She set off down the lane towards Compton Court, filling the car with the scent of tuberose and the sound of Celine Dion. As she approached the gates of Compton Court she switched to Classic FM. It wouldn't do to be heard listening to pop music.

Compton Court was as prestigious a house as the name suggested. Flappy had never been inside, but she'd seen it in photographs (once it had been featured in *Tatler* magazine with a portrait of Lady Micklethwaite riding side saddle on the cover). The perfect Georgian mansion, built in the harmoniously proportioned style of Christopher Wren, was indeed even more impressive in reality than it was in photographs. The faded red brick, tall grey-tiled roof and pretty dormer windows gave it a warm, approachable air, although the charm of the design did not in the least detract from its importance. It was, indeed, a very important-looking house. Although, as Flappy drove up and parked on the gravel in front of it, she reflected on Darnley and the fact that, even if she was paid to swap, she would never *ever* part with her more beautiful home. Darnley, she decided, was without question more beautiful.

Johnson was just as she had imagined him. Elderly, formal in both attire and demeanour, but with a humorous twinkle in his eye, as if he was quite aware of the absurdity of his position in an unsophisticated town like Badley Compton. However, he greeted Flappy and led her through the house to the garden, while Flappy's keen eye took in every exquisite detail. Hedda and two ladies were seated on brand new teak chairs, drinking glasses of wine. When she saw Flappy, Hedda jumped to her feet. 'My dear Flappy,' she said. 'How lovely to see you.' She took Flappy's hands and kissed her cold cheek. Hedda's, Flappy noticed, was plump and warm.

'You have a beautiful home,' said Flappy. She was just about to say how much more beautiful it was now than when the Micklethwaites had owned it, when Lady Micklethwaite herself turned round and smiled at her. Flappy was completely taken aback. There she was, Lady Micklethwaite, casual in a floral blouse and long cream skirt, her greying hair swept up and clipped in a loose bun, her fine English face tanned and freckled. But if Flappy was good at one thing, it was hiding shock in moments such as these.

'Phyllida,' said Flappy, for she wasn't going to let on how little she knew Lady Micklethwaite by using her title.

'Flappy,' replied Lady Micklethwaite.

'I thought you were in Spain.'

'We were, but I've come back to collect the last of our things that Eddie has kindly kept for us in the barn.'

'Oh,' said Flappy, suddenly realizing, to her horror, that these two women knew each other.

'Eddie and I were at school together,' said Lady Micklethwaite.

'Scrap was very naughty,' said Hedda with a laugh, grinning at Lady Micklethwaite, who didn't look at all like a Scrap. 'Midnight feasts and dares you wouldn't believe.'

'Eddie bet I couldn't run naked through the box garden, but I did!'

'And won a big bag of sweets, if I recall!' The two women laughed as only deeply intimate friends do.

'Hello,' said Big Mary, giving Flappy a wave from the other side of the teak table.

'Ah, Mary,' said Flappy. Never had she been so relieved to see Big Mary. She took the chair beside her and sat down.

'I'm very sad I'm not going to be around for Eddie's party,' said Lady Micklethwaite, pulling a face.

'No one is sadder than me,' said Hedda, sinking into the chair beside Lady Micklethwaite. 'But you *will* come back and there *will* be more parties. You know how I love to give parties.'

Johnson brought Flappy a glass of wine. She was very grateful for it. These two women, knowing each other so well, had unsettled her. She took a sip and tried to find a way to reassert herself. Flappy did not like to feel on the periphery of things.

'Badley Compton is all the poorer now that you have left,' said Flappy to Lady Micklethwaite. 'Who am I going to get to open the fêtes and be guest of honour at our charity luncheons?'

Lady Micklethwaite was flattered. 'Oh, I'm sure you'll find someone, Flappy,' she said. 'If anyone can, you can.'

Flappy was delighted by Lady Micklethwaite's praise, although she was right, of course. If anyone could find the appropriate person to open fêtes and be guest of honour at charity luncheons, it was Flappy.

'I'll volunteer, if you like,' said Hedda.

Before Flappy could reply that she required someone with a title, Lady Micklethwaite responded enthusiastically. 'There, you have found someone already! Eddie would be perfect. She's much grander than me.'

Flappy laughed uneasily. 'Oh, surely not,' she said.

'Of course she is,' exclaimed Lady Micklethwaite. 'Eddie's uncle was a marquess.'

This piece of information, so lightly given, took Flappy's breath away. It was bad enough that Hedda was a member of the aristocracy, but the fact that Flappy knew nothing about it, that this was the first she had heard of it, was enough to prevent her from ever breathing again. But then, like a knight in shining armour, rescuing her just when she was in dire need of being rescued, or at least distracted, was Charles.

'Charles!' exclaimed Hedda and Lady Micklethwaite in unison as he appeared round the corner.

'Hello, ladies,' he said, stopping in his tracks to take in the four faces now turning towards him. 'Hello, Mary,' he added, smiling at Hedda's niece. Then his green gaze alighted on Flappy. 'Ah, Flappy. How nice to see you. I had a good game of golf with Kenneth this morning.'

'I know you did,' said Flappy, feeling a little more like herself again. 'He said you're a jolly good player.'

'He's too kind. He was on terrific form and covered himself in glory.'

'How funny. He said the same about you.'

He turned to Lady Micklethwaite. 'Perhaps Algie would like to join us tomorrow.'

'You're playing again?' said Hedda.

Charles laughed. 'There's no stopping Kenneth.'

'He is rather obsessed,' Flappy agreed.

'Well, the course is his, isn't it,' said Big Mary. 'If I had a swimming pool named after me I think I'd use it every day as well.' Flappy thought, considering her size, that she'd do well to use a swimming pool every day.

'The Scott-Booth Golf Course,' said Charles. 'And a very fine course it is too.'

'I'm sure Algie would love to play,' said Lady Micklethwaite. He'd always been Sir Algernon to Flappy. 'You know the house we've bought in Spain is actually built on a golf course.'

Flappy was appalled to hear that. She'd thought more highly of the Micklethwaites. 'How lovely,' she gushed.

'No, it's dreadful,' said Lady Micklethwaite. 'But Algie loves it.' She looked at Hedda and smiled. 'Happy husband, happy wife, right, Eddie?'

'Yes, indeed, Scrap,' Hedda agreed. 'Now, I think it's time for bridge, don't you?'

Before they commenced their game, which was to take place in the blue drawing room (Compton Court boasted five), Flappy went to powder her nose. She didn't need to use the bathroom, but she was curious to see more of the house and requesting to use the bathroom gave her the perfect opportunity without looking like she was prying. Now she knew that Hedda's uncle was a marquess she was determined to find out who her uncle was, whether her father had been a lord, and what, if any, was *her* title. An honourable, perhaps? As she made her way through the house, behind Johnson who had been charged with escorting her to the ladies' room, everything began to fall into place. The grandeur of the house itself, from the exquisite furniture, paintings and faded Persian rugs to the family portraits and trinkets, revealed aristocratic good taste and, perhaps, heirlooms inherited from distinguished ancestors. Hedda's sense of entitlement, the way she had just plonked herself down in Flappy's seat in church, for example, and the manner in which she accepted things without so much as a thank-you, as if they were her due, indicated someone who had been brought up in a certain style. In the kind of family that had staff, such as Johnson. Flappy, as much as she was irritated, was also impressed. Hedda hadn't mentioned how grand she was, which was admirable. Flappy hated people who 'blew their own trumpet' as she called it. How much better it was to leave other people to sing one's praises and shout about one's achievements on one's behalf.

She was walking back down the corridor when Charles's voice called her name from inside one of the rooms. She stopped. 'Is that you, Charles?' she asked.

'Come over here. I want to show you something,' he said.

Flappy stepped into a study. By the look of the decoration and the use of deep, masculine greens and blacks, she could tell that it was *his* study. He was standing in front of the fireplace, surrounded by unopened cardboard boxes with the letters 'CS' in black marker pen written on the sides. 'I haven't got round to unpacking yet,' he said. 'Actually, the thought rather overwhelms me. It's a devil of a thing moving house.'

'They say it's as traumatic as a divorce,' said Flappy.

'Well, I wouldn't know,' said Charles, turning his beautiful eyes onto her and causing a fluttering feeling to tickle her belly. 'I want to show you this.' He held up a butterfly in a glass case. 'This is a very rare butterfly from Brazil. Isn't it splendid?'

'It's exquisite,' said Flappy, stepping closer to admire it. 'I don't think I've ever seen one of those before. Kenneth and I went to Brazil some years back, but I don't recall seeing one like that.'

'There are very few left in the world,' he told her. 'I wanted you to see it, because, like you, I appreciate beautiful things.'

'Do you?' she breathed.

'I do. I appreciate beautiful flowers, beautiful creatures, beautiful art and music. I think you do too.'

'Oh, I do,' said Flappy.

'And women,' he added, looking at her steadily. 'I appreciate a beautiful woman more than anything.'

Flappy felt as if a hand had just grabbed her by the throat. 'Really?' she said and her voice was suddenly dry and husky.

'You're a very beautiful woman, Flappy.' He laughed bashfully. 'But you know that. Of course you know that. You must have been told a million times.'

'Well, not a million, no,' she replied, thinking more in the hundreds, to be accurate. She wanted to add that she'd never been told it by anyone who looked like him.

'Forgive me, but I have to speak my mind. Ever since I met you in church yesterday I haven't been able to get you out of my thoughts.'

'Oh,' said Flappy, watching his sensual mouth move as he delivered those beautiful words.

'I know we're both married, and what I'm saying is completely out of order, but I cannot help myself.'

Flappy didn't know what to say. She stood staring at him in astonishment, pleased and a little frightened too. She wasn't sure she was going to be able to help herself either.

'I should leave you to your bridge,' he said, putting the butterfly down.

'Yes, I suppose you'd better.' Although Flappy would have much preferred to stay talking to *him*.

'Hedda will be wondering where you are.'

'I'll say I got lost.'

He flashed a dazzling smile and Flappy almost swooned. 'I will tell her *I* found you. Come.'

Flappy followed him. As they approached the blue drawing room he turned to her and added, 'I'm so very happy I've come to live in Badley Compton.'

Chapter 5

Flappy was in a fluster. She did not want to return home in such a state. Kenneth would suspect something. Not that anything had happened. It hadn't. Just a little flirtation. No harm in that, was there, Flappy thought as she pulled into a farm entrance and took a few deep breaths to calm her nerves, which were really quite frantic. In fact, she couldn't remember a time when her nerves had been so agitated.

What a tremendous evening it had been, she reflected, sitting in the car. She'd played exceedingly good bridge. Big Mary, who she had partnered, had said she was 'on fire'. Well, she'd been right about that. Flappy felt as if her entire body was on fire. Every inch of her. She'd never felt more alive. Ever. Hedda had been so impressed with her skill that she'd asked her to become a regular member of her bridge team, and Lady Micklethwaite had invited her and Kenneth to stay with them in Spain. Carried on a wave of goodwill, Flappy had climbed into her car at the end of the evening and turned to the hostess. In her most gracious voice, she had said she would love Hedda to replace Lady Micklethwaite in the opening of events and being guest of honour at her charity luncheons. 'The honour will be all mine,' Hedda had replied and Flappy had flashed her most enchanting smile and given a royal wave as she drove off down the drive. The evening had been an enormous success.

However, her most enduring memory of the evening was of Charles. The moment when he had looked deep into her eyes and told her, in a voice so low that she was the only person to hear it, that he was very happy he'd moved to Badley Compton. Well, fancy that!

Flappy believed she was in love. She wasn't sure she'd ever been in love before. Of course, she'd fancied men in her youth, and Kenneth, when she'd first met him across the gloves counter in Harrods (her first job), had certainly caused something mildly exciting to stir inside her, but it was nothing near the commotion Charles induced. This was different, very different. There was a terrible urgency about this feeling. A sense of need and, dare she admit it, an uncontrollable sexual desire. Yes, it was indeed sexual desire with all its hot flushes and aching loins. Nothing remotely close to it had ever taken hold of Flappy. She'd read about it (in Charity Chance's novels), heard other people talking about it (Madge after a few glasses of wine could be surprisingly vulgar), and seen it played out in movies, but never had she truly experienced it. She recognized that now because all she could think about was lying naked in his arms and of him caressing her, every gorgeous inch of her, with a slow and gentle touch.

By the time she reached Darnley she had acquired a

semblance of calm. Kenneth was in the television room watching a replay of *Poirot*. 'How was your bridge game?' he asked, pressing the pause button on the television and reluctantly drawing himself away.

'Lovely,' said Flappy breezily. 'Just lovely. Lady Micklethwaite was there and has invited us to Spain. Isn't that nice of her?'

'Very nice,' Kenneth agreed.

'They live on a golf course. Literally on it. One wouldn't imagine them to live in a place like that, would one?' she added.

At the mention of a golf course Kenneth perked up. 'A golf course in Spain? How splendid!'

'Oh, and Charles invited Sir Algernon to play golf with you tomorrow.'

Kenneth's small eyes brightened with enthusiasm. 'That's good,' he said. 'I think Sir Algernon is a top player.'

'You know Hedda and Phyllida are old school friends. Isn't that a surprise? And Hedda's uncle was a marquess. I was wondering, as I drove home tonight, what her title must be, because, if her uncle was a marquess, then his brother, her father, must have been a lord, wouldn't you say? In which case, she must be an honourable. Her brother Harry must have been an honourable too. How extraordinary. I should think Hedda has a different mother to Harry because he was in his eighties when he died and Hedda can't be much older than me. I must find out. I've asked her to take Lady Micklethwaite's place and open our events. Isn't that a good idea? Had she not been an aristocrat I would not have considered her, but as she is, it's appropriate that she should do her duty for the town. Titles are all very well, but they come with a great deal of responsibility and one must give back, mustn't one?' Flappy caught her breath. All this excitement was too much. 'Hedda has staff, you know,' she continued, although Kenneth was only half listening. 'A butler called Johnson and a cook called Mrs Ellis, who cooked the most delicious dinner for the four of us. I'm not sure what happened to Charles. He must have gone out for he didn't join us at the table. It was strictly women only.' She sighed, regretting that part. 'But when I did manage to talk to him, briefly, he said what a good game of golf he had had with you. Isn't that nice, darling?'

'Very,' said Kenneth.

'I think we're going to like having the Harvey-Smiths in Badley Compton.'

Kenneth nodded and pressed 'play' on the remote. *Poirot* resumed and Kenneth's attention was lost.

Flappy went to the kitchen and poured herself a large glass of white wine. Then she went upstairs and ran a bath. While she lolled in the warm scented water, sipping Chardonnay, she let her mind drift once again to Charles.

The following morning Flappy hosted a meeting for the Harvest Festival tea in her exquisite drawing room. Really, every time she walked into that room she appreciated how truly exquisite it was. All taupes and creams and good taste. *Lots* of good taste. Indeed, it could not be denied that there was simply so much good taste at Darnley.

Esther, Madge, Mabel and Sally were the core members of all Flappy's committees – they could not have refused even if they'd wanted to, such was their terror of Flappy's disapproval – but Flappy enjoyed including a few men from time to time, so that their meetings didn't grow stale. For the Harvest Festival committee, there was the vicar, Reverend Willis, who was sensible and pragmatic, and Gerald Pott, unmarried, in his early sixties, with ginger hair and soft brown eyes, who was not. Gerald was Flappy's decorator. He was flamboyant, effete, and thought the world of her, which was his greatest qualification. Today he found her somewhat distracted. 'Flappy darling, has your sharp eye found some imperfection in the room that might need correcting?' he asked. It was always worth a try. Flappy had loads of money and was easily persuaded to redecorate.

'What do you mean, Gerald?' Flappy asked.

'You're *distrait*.'

'*Moi*?' Flappy frowned, but not so much that it disturbed the smooth skin on her forehead.

'Poor Flappy, you do too much,' said Mabel. 'That's the trouble. But now you have Persephone, you should step back a bit. As you always say, you can't be all things to all people.'

'But one must try,' said Flappy earnestly. 'The town depends on me, you see. I've always had a strong sense of duty. Those to whom much is given, much will be required, *n'est-ce pas*?'

Reverend Willis, who was quite happy to allow Flappy to do all the talking, reserving his right to long soliloquies in the pulpit only, smiled in a vicarish way, and said, 'Luke

12:48. A wise quote indeed. Badley Compton appreciates all the hard work you do, Flappy. It's a fine thing to have such community spirit. I'm very glad you've employed a bright young person to share the load.' He looked at Persephone and gave her a vicarish smile too.

Persephone had made everyone tea and coffee, produced a plate of digestive biscuits and taken notes throughout the meeting. She had spent the evening before coming up with decorating ideas for the marquee, as Flappy was going to host the tea on her lawn on the Sunday afternoon. She'd thought of making candleholders out of miniature pumpkins and arranging hay bales in circles for seating. Sheaves of wheat would look pretty and nostalgic, and toffee apples for the children were always popular. She'd given the list to Flappy prior to the meeting and Flappy had been delighted. However, it had come as something of a surprise when Flappy had claimed those ideas as her own. Persephone was powerless to do anything but watch, helplessly, as Flappy took credit for her hard work. 'There,' she said after listing them. '*I've* come up with the ideas, who's going to carry them out?'

'I can make the candles,' Madge volunteered. 'I once did a candle-making course, many years ago. I could give them a cinnamon scent. Do you think that would be nice?'

Flappy didn't. 'It's not Christmas, Madge,' she said. 'I think a woody smell would be more appropriate, or something more relevant to harvest time, like blackberries or apples.'

Madge nodded. 'Of course, you're quite right, Flappy. We don't want people thinking Christmas has come early, do we?' She laughed nervously.

'Anyone else?' said Flappy, looking at each one in turn and hoping to draw out volunteers. She certainly wasn't intending to do anything herself.

'I can produce the hay bales,' said Esther. 'We have a barn full of them.'

'Good, you could perhaps bring one of your horses to give the children rides.'

'I'll bring the donkey.'

'You have a donkey?' said Sally.

'Two. Rescue donkeys. Very friendly, especially when you produce the odd carrot.' Esther laughed cheerfully.

'I'll take care of the tea,' said Mabel. 'I'll ask Big Mary to supply cakes.'

'Perhaps she could theme them,' Persephone suggested. 'Cupcakes with pumpkins on.'

'Save that one for Halloween, dear,' said Flappy. 'She could decorate them with ears of wheat. That would be more appropriate. Remember, it's harvest not Halloween. The odd pumpkin here and there is all very well, but if we have too many people will get confused and think it's Halloween come early.'

Persephone smiled. 'I'm sure they'll all know it's not Halloween,' she said.

Flappy did not smile. 'You'd be surprised, Persephone, how clueless people can be.'

'I couldn't possibly let anyone else loose with the decoration,' said Gerald. 'Persephone can be my assistant. I'll need an extra pair of hands. Can you spare her?' he asked Flappy.

'Excellent idea,' said Flappy. She turned to Persephone. 'The secret to being a success in life is to take opportunities to learn when they are given. Gerald is one of the finest decorators in the country. I mean, just look around you and admire what he has done for me. We're a good team, aren't we, Gerald?'

Gerald had known Flappy for more than twenty years and was used to her taking credit when credit wasn't due. 'We are, Flappy,' he said. 'I think it's time we started another project, don't you?'

Flappy narrowed her eyes, trying to think of a room that needed redecorating, but couldn't find one. The rooms were all perfect and complete at Darnley. Then her sharp mind swooped onto the picturesque little cottage at the bottom of the garden that had once served as an artist's studio when Flappy had gone through her painting stage (she had been brilliantly talented as one would expect, but in the end she had simply run out of time, being so incredibly busy). It was adorable with two upstairs bedrooms and a kitchen–sitting room downstairs with large sash windows that let in the light. She didn't think she'd take up painting again – there was only room in the world for one Hockney, after all, but perhaps it could be used for something else? And then an idea popped into her head, as ideas tended to do just when she needed them: a meditation room.

'I couldn't agree with you more, Gerald,' she said. 'And I have just the thing in mind.'

Kenneth returned from the golf club at lunchtime in high spirits. He'd played with Sir Algernon and Charles and exceeded himself, scoring a fluky hole in one. He sat down to lunch on the terrace, where Karen had laid the table in the shade, and poured himself a glass of wine. He poured one for Flappy too, although she didn't usually drink during the day because it made her sleepy – and Flappy didn't have hours to waste on siestas in the afternoons. 'I have a favour to ask you,' said Kenneth, tucking into the quiche, buttered new potatoes and salad that Karen had made.

'Oh?' said Flappy, already unwilling. The last time he'd asked her for a favour she'd rashly agreed to invite a golfing friend of his to supper with his new, indecently young wife, and regretted it. The girl had compared Flappy to her mother and had the gall to tell her how much younger her mother looked since her facelift. No, Flappy did not feel inclined to agree to whatever absurd request Kenneth was about to put before her.

'Charles has asked whether he might have the use of our swimming pool.'

Well, this was an entirely different matter. 'Really?' said Flappy, hiding her excitement. If there was one thing Flappy was good at, it was hiding her emotions when emotions were better off hidden.

'Yes, you see, they don't have a swimming pool at Compton Court.'

'You would have thought they would have one, wouldn't you?' said Flappy, rather pleased that *they* had a pool and Hedda didn't.

'Charles has bad knees, so he has to be careful how he exercises. Swimming is the best thing for him.'

'I'm sure it is,' said Flappy, flushing a little at the thought of Charles in swimming trunks.

'He was a member of the Harbour Club in London—'

'Of course he was,' Flappy interrupted with satisfaction. The Harbour Club was just the place a person like Charles Harvey-Smith would frequent.

'I know you don't like people using our facilities, I mean, it's good of you to open the gardens in June, but Charles is a friend and—'

'He can use it,' she said.

Kenneth raised his eyebrows and smiled in surprise. 'He can?'

'Absolutely,' said Flappy. 'He must get his exercise, after all.'

'I'll tell him. He'll be very pleased.'

'Good. You know, when one is lucky enough to have a swimming pool, it's only right that one should share it.'

Kenneth put his hand on his wife's. He really was very grateful that she'd agreed. 'You're such a generous person, darling,' he said. 'Always thinking about other people. I don't think there's a person within a hundred miles who is as selfless as you.'

Flappy was beside herself at the thought of Charles coming to use the swimming pool. She immediately went to check that it was pristine with clean towels, soap and shampoo in the shower – it wouldn't do for word to get back to Hedda that Flappy was careless with hygiene. However, as beautiful as the swimming pool was, Flappy never used it herself. She didn't like to get wet, unless she was in the bath, or in the Caribbean in unbearably hot temperatures. It was a chore to have to dry her hair – she had a blow-dry twice a week in town which saved her from ever having to do it herself. The trouble was she had such thick and lustrous hair (really, it was impossibly thick and lustrous) the task was arduous and Flappy didn't have the time. Although, she was the first to acknowledge how very *very* lucky she was to be so follicly blessed.

When Flappy asked Kenneth when Charles was going to come, the answer was, 'This very afternoon, if that's okay with you, darling.' Flappy responded coolly, giving nothing away, then hurried upstairs to repair her make-up and squirt perfume on her neck. She knew she was being foolish. If Flappy knew one thing, it was when she was being foolish, but she also knew that it was something she was unable to help. Dizzy with expectation and enjoying feeling like a teenager again, or perhaps for the first time because when she'd been a teenager she'd always felt like a forty-year-old, she went into the garden to pick flowers. When Charles's shiny black Bentley rolled up in front of the house, Flappy made her way slowly round from the croquet lawn, in sunglasses and straw trilby, carrying a pretty bouquet of late-summer flowers. She beamed a smile. 'Oh, Charles, you've caught me slaving away in the garden,' she said, the scent of tuberose overpowering the more subtle scent of pinks and lilies. 'But it's a treat to see you.'

He returned her smile, sending her a little off balance.

'You're very kind to let me use your pool. It's the one thing I was looking for when we were searching for a home, but then we fell in love with Compton and that was that. No pool.'

'You're welcome to use ours whenever you like. Really, Kenneth barely uses it and I do my lengths every morning at dawn.'

He looked at her with admiration. 'You're one of those early risers, are you?'

'I have to be,' she replied. 'Otherwise, I simply can't get everything done. The days just aren't long enough.'

He went to the boot and lifted out a chic leather holdall. It looked very Ralph Lauren, Flappy thought. How appropriate that Charles should have a Ralph Lauren holdall. She led him into the hall. 'Welcome to our humble abode,' she said, hoping he would notice the Jonathan Yeo portraits. She lingered a moment to give him time and then, just as she knew he would, he looked up at the wall.

'Gosh!' he exclaimed. 'What splendid portraits.' But he wasn't looking at Kenneth's. He shook his head in wonder. 'You look beautiful, Flappy.'

'Oh, it's just a bit of fun,' she said, waving the secateurs. 'Jonathan insisted. I only wanted him to paint Kenneth, but he demanded to paint me as well. Kenneth wouldn't let me decline, so, there it is. *Moi.*' She laughed. 'Quite charming, I think.'

'It's more than charming. It's a masterpiece.'

She laughed again, because everything Charles said made her want to laugh with joy. 'No one has ever called me a masterpiece before.'

'I doubt that very much. A woman like you must be tired of being called a masterpiece.'

'I don't think I'd ever tire of that.'

She led him through the house so that he could see as much of it as possible. As she'd hoped, he recognized her good taste at once. 'You have a stunning home, Flappy.'

'Thank you. I'm glad you like it, because there was very little thought put into it. I just, kind of, threw it together.'

'Well, the effect is impressive.'

'I got lucky. It fell into place rather nicely. A total fluke.'

She led him into the kitchen so that she could put the flowers into a vase. 'Would you like a cup of tea or a glass of something?'

'A glass of water would be nice,' he replied. 'It's a warm day, isn't it?'

'It's a lovely day. Usually, I'm too busy to enjoy days like these, but this afternoon I had a couple of hours free to spend in the garden. It's hard work, but it's pleasurable, isn't it? To be out in nature.' She sighed. 'I do love nature.'

Charles was looking at her with a dreamy look in his eyes when Kenneth walked in. 'Ah, Charles,' he said.

'Hello, Kenneth,' Charles replied, bringing his gaze into focus. 'Your lovely wife is looking after me.'

'She's good at that.' Kenneth smiled appreciatively at his wife.

Flappy put the vase of flowers on the table. 'There, don't they look nice? Summer's not over yet.' She turned to Charles. 'Your party is going to be the last of the summer.'

'I think it is. Hedda's been busy planning it.'

'We're very much looking forward to it,' said Kenneth.

'Yes, we are,' agreed Flappy. 'Come, let me show you to the pool.'

'Don't worry, Flappy. I'll show him if you like,' said Kenneth.

'No, no. I'll do it, darling,' she insisted casually. 'I need to fetch something down there anyway.'

Flappy took Charles through the house to the swimming pool, which Kenneth and Flappy had built when they bought the house some thirty years ago. It was a light, airy room with lots of windows and glass doors opening onto the rose garden and a terrace where Flappy occasionally entertained friends for lunch. Charles was admiring of the pool, especially the mosaic hippo grinning up through the turquoise water. 'Flappy,' he said and there was a seriousness to his tone that made her turn round with a pang of anxiety.

'Yes?' she replied.

'I need to make a confession.'

'You do?'

'Yes.' He looked bashful.

She wanted to take his face in her hands and kiss it. 'What have you done?'

He looked at her steadily, those sea-green eyes sheepish suddenly. 'I don't have a problem with my knees.'

'You don't?' Flappy's heart began to accelerate.

'No. I don't need to use the pool for physiotherapy.' He shrugged. 'I don't need to use it at all.'

'Oh?'

'I needed an excuse to see *you*.'

71

The 'Oh' that escaped Flappy's lips was more of a breath.

'I'm sorry, Flappy, to put you in this awkward position, but I cannot help myself. I have fallen in love with you.'

Flappy thought she might swoon. But if she was good at one thing, it was gathering her strength when she needed it most. She looked straight into his eyes and sighed. 'Oh, Charles.'

Chapter 6

Flappy was not the sort of woman to plunge into something as dramatic as an extramarital affair without a great deal of thought – and consideration for her husband of whom she had only a few minor complaints. So it came as an enormous surprise to her when, abandoned suddenly by her customary self-control, she allowed Charles to kiss her.

The kiss itself was rash enough, but the fact that he did it in the middle of the pool house where glass windows and doors exposed them like goldfish to any gardener just happening to walk by or, indeed, to Kenneth himself, who liked to wander around the gardens and ponder on his success, was downright stupid. But neither Flappy nor Charles were thinking rationally. Fuelled by an uncontainable passion that turned their brains to mush, they considered no one but themselves.

Flappy had never been kissed like that before, not ever. Sure, Kenneth, in his day, had been an adequate kisser, and prior to him she had endured the odd kiss at parties, but Flappy had never really liked being kissed. Kisses were too wet, too messy and 'bestial'. There, that word again; sex and kisses reduced the human being to the level of an animal and that, up until now, had been beneath Flappy's dignity and avoided where possible.

Charles's kiss was different. There was something delightfully erotic about it that gave her feelings in all the places she knew she ought to have feelings, but never had. Naughty places. Places where lurked the beast in her nature, up until this moment safely harnessed and ignored. But now, in a frenzy of unleashing, the beast was set free. They hurried into the changing room, breathless and overheating, and tore at their clothes. Charles put his hand up her shirt to feel her breasts and Flappy unbuckled his belt. With deft hands they explored each other like teenagers at a ball. And then he was inside her and Flappy was aware only of the delicious, intoxicating sensations occurring in every corner of her body. Out of her mind with pleasure she forgot herself, her ambitions, her petty wants and desires, and was aware only of Charles and what he was doing to her.

Flappy was undone. The control for which she was so highly respected in the community had melted like ice in sunshine. 'We should not have done this,' she said as she buttoned up her shirt and pulled on her trousers.

'We shouldn't have,' Charles agreed, slipping into his swimming shorts. 'But we couldn't help ourselves.'

'I think a swim will be a very good thing,' she said.

'Yes, I do need to cool down.'

'We mustn't do that again.'

Charles looked at her with those beautiful eyes and grinned. 'But you know we will.'

Flappy lifted her chin. 'I can excuse a moment of madness, but two is reckless.'

He wound his hand round her neck and kissed her on the lips. 'Then I'm afraid I have to admit that I'm *very* reckless, Flappy.'

Flappy left him to do his lengths and hurried upstairs, hoping not to bump into Persephone or Kenneth. Fortunately, Kenneth was watching the golf on television and Persephone had driven into town to buy the wine Flappy had requested for her wine-tasting dinner on Thursday, which was what her informal supper with the Harvey-Smiths and the Willises had become. Persephone was to write a report on each of the wines so that Flappy could show off her knowledge. It would also give her a good opportunity to show off her languages too. She had requested Spanish, French and Italian wine. '*Bueno, bon, buono!*'

In the safety of her bedroom Flappy went into the bathroom and locked the door. After spraying perfume all over her body, she scrutinized her face in the mirror. Did she look different? Was there perhaps something wild in her eyes that might give her away? Could the beast be *seen*? Satisfied (if a little disappointed) that she looked just like she always did, she went into her bedroom and sat at her vanity table. She brushed her hair, reapplied her make-up (although Flappy wore very little, for being a natural beauty she did not need face paint to fake it) and once again studied her face. Getting old was a tragedy, she conceded. She knew she looked good for her age, but she was still her age, and ageing. There was no avoiding it. Of course one could opt for surgery, but

Flappy loathed the idea of going under the surgeon's knife for something so banal. She'd be jolly miffed if she died on the operating table simply because she'd wanted to look a little younger. And besides, no one ended up looking younger, they ended up looking lifted. No one ever said, 'Doesn't she look good,' they always said, 'Hasn't she had a lot of work done?' *Non*, Flappy would never have a facelift. She would grow old gracefully, but still, it could not be helped, growing old was a pity.

Flappy lay against the pillows on her bed and closed her eyes. What she had just done in the pool house was unforgivable, really, considering how attentive and kind Kenneth was. He didn't deserve to be a cuckold. Sure, one could complain that he had a lover of his own, but the golf course didn't really count. Flappy was not jealous of the golf course. In fact, it suited her. She didn't want to see too much of Kenneth. However, she felt a growing sense of guilt. She wallowed in it for a moment, thinking of Kenneth's round face going all pink with hurt, and feeling bad that she'd caused it. But, it was hard to immerse herself in guilt when the pleasure of that moment was so overpowering. Her guilt was quickly forgotten as she lay on the bed and relived every delicious moment of her encounter with Charles.

Flappy did not want to compare Charles to Kenneth. That was unfair and unkind. But after struggling with the impulse to do so, she gave up the fight and allowed herself to measure up both men. After all, Flappy's mind was so alert and so busy it was impossible to rein it in when it had decided to gallop ahead. Apart from the fact that Charles was handsome and

Kenneth was not, there were other differences that weighed in Charles's favour. He was tall, Kenneth was short; Charles was slim and athletic, Kenneth was portly and unfit; Charles had lots of thick grey hair, Kenneth was bald and shiny on top; Charles had the most astonishing eyes, Kenneth's were just eyes. In fact, if one considered the food chain, Charles was a white tiger and Kenneth was a toad, which, as it happened, was the nickname she'd coined for him in the early days of their marriage.

Flappy loved Kenneth. Well, she thought she must do because they'd been married for forty years and been perfectly content. Flappy had never looked at another man and Kenneth had only ever looked at his golf clubs. Kenneth had always given Flappy everything she wanted and, at times, she'd asked for quite a lot. He'd never said no. In fact, now that she thought about it, she didn't think he'd ever said no in all the years they'd been married. It helped that he was enormously rich, of course. Buying Flappy a new car or the house in the Algarve, or indulging her desire to redecorate rooms that didn't need redecorating, was nothing for him, but it did not detract from the fact that he was generous. Very generous. Flappy didn't know whether Charles was generous or acquiescent so they were incomparable in that department. The bottom line was, Kenneth was easy to live with. He was uncomplicated, jovial and liked everyone – and everyone liked him. There was no doubt about it, Flappy acknowledged, Kenneth was a very nice man.

But Kenneth had never lit Flappy's internal wick. Until Charles appeared at church on Sunday Flappy wasn't sure she even had a wick. She'd devoured Charity Chance's novels – and plenty of other romantic books besides – and assumed that these women with raging internal flames of passion were not like her. She'd assumed, and had been quite certain about it, that she was simply a more spiritual woman. A woman so enlightened that she was above the primitive desires of more earthly women. Many years ago, she'd had a chat with a priest she'd met in Ireland who told her that sexual abstinence was not meant to be the struggle so many men of the cloth find it to be, for a truly spiritual person is of a higher consciousness and feels no sexual urges at all; he is quite simply above it. Flappy had had an epiphany. She'd accepted that her lack of sexual drive was not a failing on her part but a massive blessing. It merely meant that she was closer to God.

The fact that she had discovered that she did have a wick, after all, and that the wick had been lit and blazed with a flame far brighter than any of Charity Chance's heroines', was a trifle alarming. She'd rather celebrated her elevated spiritual status. But she realized now that she wasn't an enlightened soul with a higher consciousness than other women, she was a sexual creature with sexual desires, just like everyone else. It made her ordinary, and if there was one thing Flappy did not like, it was being ordinary.

She wouldn't do it again.

She would resist Charles's advances, there would obviously be more, because hadn't he said himself that he had fallen in love with her? Well, she couldn't blame him for that, a man's heart was what it was, but she *could* take the moral high ground. She shouldn't have done it in the first place, but it wasn't too late to put it right. They hadn't been caught. No one knew but them. It could remain a secret, a *delicious* secret, that would put a smile on her face whenever she thought about it, and perhaps allow them to enjoy the odd knowing glance every now and then, which would be exciting. But it couldn't happen again. Perhaps, she thought with rising excitement, God had put this temptation in her path to teach her a lesson in resistance. So, she had slipped up the first time, but the opportunity would soon arise for her to show that she could follow Jesus's example and resist temptation when temptation presented itself.

Satisfied that she hadn't fallen from Grace, and a little excited that she was, after all, a woman with a capacity for sexual pleasure, Flappy climbed off the bed and skipped breezily downstairs to see if Persephone was back with the wine.

Persephone was in the kitchen talking to Kenneth. The bottles of wine were standing in a neat row on the island and the two of them were looking at them. Indeed, Kenneth was holding a bottle and reading the label. 'Ah, there you are, darling,' he said when he saw Flappy. 'I thought you were having a rest.'

'A rest! Me? Goodness, no. I haven't time for a rest.' She sighed. 'How I would adore to have time for a rest.'

'Here are the bottles for your wine-tasting, Mrs Scott-Booth,' said Persephone. 'I managed to get six of the finest vintages.'

'You clever girl,' said Flappy. She watched the two of

79

them carefully to see if they had observed a change in her that she hadn't spotted in the mirror, but neither seemed to have noticed anything.

'Genius idea to have a wine-tasting,' said Kenneth.

'I thought so too,' said Flappy.

'It was very kind of you to allow Charles to use the pool,' he added, giving his wife a grateful smile.

'*Fa niente*, darling. It's the least I can do to make Hedda and Charles feel welcome. And we are so *so* lucky to have a pool.'

The following morning Gerald came round to have a look at the cottage and to talk to Persephone about the decoration for the Harvest Festival tea. 'You're glowing,' he said to Flappy as the three of them walked across the croquet lawn, through the arboretum and round the lily pond to the pretty white cottage with the thatched roof that was partially hidden behind a tall beech hedge.

'It's adorable,' exclaimed Persephone when she saw it. 'It's like something out of a fairy tale.'

'"Hansel and Gretel", I always think,' said Flappy.

'Without the witch,' added Gerald.

'Oh, she's in the oven!' laughed Flappy. Gerald grinned. He was good at making Flappy laugh – as well as spending money.

Flappy opened the gate and they walked down the gravel path to the front door, which was painted a tasteful blue-grey. 'I'm going to use this as a meditation room. A place where I can come for peace and quiet because, as you know, my life is so busy.' She opened the door. 'What do you think, Gerald?'

Gerald stepped into the middle of the sitting room, put his hands on his hips and looked around. The room was larger than one would imagine from the outside with a pretty fireplace and a low ceiling supported by old beams. 'It has a wonderful energy, Flappy,' he said. 'We can really work with this.'

'Good. I was thinking a statue of Buddha, a little fountain perhaps, lots of candles . . . '

'A shrine,' said Gerald. 'If you're going to have a statue of Buddha, you must have a shrine.'

'Of course,' Flappy agreed. 'One can't have a meditation room without a shrine. Persephone, can you find me some music, you know, something soothing to listen to as I'm med-itating. One always needs music, don't you think, Gerald.'

'I like the sound of rain and birds,' said Gerald.

'See if you can find some music with rain and birds, Persephone,' said Flappy.

'Yes, Mrs Scott-Booth,' she replied and dutifully wrote it down on her pad.

Flappy showed them upstairs. The bedrooms were pretty with beds so high you had to climb onto them. Flappy's busy mind stilled for a moment and an image floated before her eyes. She and Charles, in that bed, making love to the sound of cooing pigeons and roosting songbirds. She caught her breath.

'It looks a little tired in here,' said Gerald, scrunching up his nose. 'How about we give it a lift, Flappy?'

Flappy was brought sharply back to the present. 'What did you say, Gerald?'

He laughed. 'You were miles away.'

'I was wondering what we could do with this room,' she lied.

'That's what I'm thinking. It could do with a little facelift.'

'Yes, let's freshen it up. I always assumed that at least one of my daughters might want the cottage as a weekend house or a holiday home, but then both of them married and went to live on the other side of the world. Imagine that? Out of all four children, not one of them lives in this country.'

'Such a shame,' said Gerald.

'But I have a wonderful relationship with them. I'm so *so* lucky to get on well with them all. Every year Kenneth flies them to the Caribbean for Christmas, husbands and wives and children – you can imagine what an exhausting enterprise it is – not to mention expensive. I'm so spoilt. They *adore* me. I'm so *so* lucky to be adored by my children. I know plenty of parents who never see their offspring, or are ignored and discarded like unwanted furniture. *Non*, mine are very attentive.'

'I'll put together a board for each room, Flappy,' said Gerald. He clapped his hands. 'What fun. We love a project, don't we!'

'We do,' said Flappy, wondering why she suddenly felt a little sad.

'Did you ever think of renting it out?' asked Persephone.

Flappy was appalled. The idea was an abhorrence. 'Goodness, no,' she exclaimed, forgetting her sadness and feeling only repellence. 'I can't think of anything worse than having strangers living at the bottom of my garden.' She inhaled through dilated nostrils. A deep, cleansing breath. 'Find me a guru, Persephone,' she added. 'There must be a spiritual teacher around somewhere who can come and teach me to meditate.'

Persephone wrote it in her pad. 'I'm sure I can find some-one,' she said.

Flappy envisaged the sitting room full of her friends, sitting cross-legged on the floor in front of the Buddha, chanting 'Om'. Then she saw Charles taking her hand and leading her upstairs. If she was going to resist him she needed to be strong. 'Find someone quickly,' she said to Persephone. 'There's no time to lose.'

It was early evening when the portable telephone rang. Flappy was in the garden, lying on a reclining chair, reading a magazine. She waited for it to ring eight times, then picked it up. 'Darnley Manor, Flappy Scott-Booth speaking.'

'Flappy, it's Mabel. I have news.'

'I'm all ears,' said Flappy, putting down the magazine.

'Hedda is the one in the marriage with money.'

Flappy sat up and took off her reading glasses. 'What do you mean?'

'Well, Big Mary told John that Hedda and Harry's father was very rich. As rich as Croesus, apparently. Charles was an actor when Hedda met him. He had nothing. Not two pennies to rub together, she said. Hedda's money bought

Compton Court. Isn't that interesting? I thought you'd like to know.'

'Well, that's just what *I* thought,' said Flappy, who didn't like to appear ignorant of anything. 'Her uncle was a marquess, you know, Lady Micklethwaite told me herself, so her father must have been a lord, if I'm not wrong, which I rarely am. You can tell by the way Hedda conducts herself that she comes from a rich and important family. However, I didn't imagine Charles to have been an actor,' she conceded, giving Mabel the chance to feel very pleased with herself for telling Flappy something she didn't know. 'Very interesting indeed, Mabel.' Flappy imagined Charles as Sean Connery, chasing baddies in a James Bond film. He'd have been very good at that, she thought.

'John also found out that Hedda and Harry were only half-siblings.'

'That's just what I thought,' said Flappy again. 'There's such a big age difference between them.'

'Apparently, Hedda's father was in his seventies when Hedda was born, with a new wife forty years his junior.'

'Disgusting,' said Flappy.

'I agree,' said Mabel, who always did. 'Disgusting.'

'John's picked up some interesting facts,' Flappy continued, wondering what else Big Mary had told him.

'He's in her café at least twice a day, for his morning coffee and afternoon tea. As you know, it's the place where you hear all the gossip.'

'Did Big Mary say what films Charles acted in?' Again the image of Sean Connery with a gun floated before her eyes.

'She just mentioned an advert for Daks in the seventies.'

'Daks?' said Flappy.

'You know, the clothing company.'

Flappy laughed. 'No, no, I'm sure that's not right. Charles would never do a commercial for a clothing company. Tell John to go back and find out what films he's been in. I imagine he was a bit of a Roger Moore or a Sean Connery in his day.' She sighed with satisfaction. 'Yes, that's much more like Charles.'

When she put down the telephone the image of Charles in a pair of beige flares and a brown shirt came out of nowhere and settled in her mind. The more she tried to get rid of it the more it refused to budge.

There was only one thing for it. She'd have to ask him herself.

Chapter 7

Flappy had worked tirelessly all day, telling Persephone and Karen what to do. It was imperative that Darnley was shown off to its best advantage so that Hedda and Charles could appreciate its splendour. It didn't matter about the vicar and his wife because they'd seen it so many times before; their appreciation was a given.

The round table was laid in the dining room with Flappy's best blue-and-white place mats which she'd bought in Florence, fine crystal glasses, heavy silver cutlery and bone china plates. There was a striking display of blue hydrangeas in the centre, candles in silver tumblers and indigo linen napkins laid neatly beside each place. The effect was quite stunning, Flappy thought, as she swept a critical eye over the room, making sure Persephone and Karen had carried out her orders to the letter. Blue and white was so tasteful. Indeed, Darnley itself was a study in good taste and class, Flappy thought, straightening the odd knife here and the odd napkin there.

Karen had been cooking for most of the afternoon. Flappy

had been very specific. She'd requested a starter from Spain, a main course from France and a dessert from Italy – and please, *niente di* tiramisu. Tiramisu, in Flappy's opinion, was very common. When Karen had come up with her suggestions, Flappy was dissatisfied. The trouble was, she told her, Italians just weren't dessert people. They might boast the best language, one of the most ancient cultures, the most beautiful buildings, the sunniest climate, the prettiest countryside and the most delicious food, but they fell short on desserts. There was no denying it: Italian desserts were sparse. So, Flappy changed the order to a Spanish starter, an Italian main course and a French dessert, followed by cheese – French again, they had a wonderful nose for cheese. The result was very pleasing indeed.

Flappy had invited her guests for eight o'clock. It did not surprise her when Graham and Joan arrived on the dot of eight. Joan was aware of Flappy's interpretation of the word 'informal', and was suitably dressed in a yellow floral dress and yellow jacket, a pair of sensible pumps on her feet. Joan was a sweet-looking woman with short brown hair, bright hazel eyes and the crinkly skin of a woman who believed that anything more than Pears soap was an unnecessary extravagance. Graham was more animated than his mousey wife. His face was always winning with a smile, a twinkle in his pale blue eyes and a rosy glow on his cheeks. But then he was the spiritual leader of his community, Flappy reasoned. It would not do to have a dull vicar or the church would be empty.

Flappy, who had taken a great deal of trouble over her

outfit, which reflected a touch of France, swept into the hall to greet them. '*Bonsoir*, Graham,' she trilled, shaking his hand (it was not done to kiss the vicar). 'You're wonderfully punctual, as always.'

'We have no reason to be late,' he replied in his calm, vicarish voice. 'We only live five minutes away, after all.'

'Joan,' said Flappy, kissing her on the cheek and smelling talcum powder and violets. 'How lovely to see you.'

'Thank you for inviting us, Flappy,' said Joan, who found Flappy rather terrifying and therefore never dared speak beyond the usual platitudes.

'Do come through to the drawing room. We're having a wine-tasting evening tonight. Such fun to compare wines from different parts of the world.'

'How lovely,' said Joan.

'Inspired,' said Graham, which coming from the vicar was high praise indeed.

Kenneth was in the drawing room. 'Hello,' he said in a jolly tone of voice, for Kenneth loved people and was always happy to see them. 'Now, I have a very good wine here. It's Italian. Would you like a glass?'

'Thank you, I'd love one. How lovely,' said Joan, who was not afraid of Kenneth.

'How nice, thank you,' echoed the vicar.

Flappy did not bother to show off her knowledge about wine to Graham and Joan. There was no point. She did not need to impress *them*. She'd wait until Hedda and Charles arrived and then she'd repeat what she'd learned by heart that afternoon. 'May we look around the garden?' asked Joan, keen to please her hostess, who she knew was deeply proud of her garden. Flappy, however, was not as pleased as Joan had hoped. She'd rather have waited for Hedda and Charles. Fortunately, just as they were about to set off, the sound of wheels crunching on gravel alerted them to the arrival of their other, more important guests. 'I'll go,' said Kenneth, heading for the door.

'We'll be outside,' Flappy called, now stepping through the French doors with enthusiasm.

A few minutes later Charles and Hedda were striding across the lawn, wine glasses in hand, followed by Kenneth. Hedda had not dressed up. She was wearing a pair of ordinary trousers and a shirt. However, Flappy's disapproval was immediately softened by the pleasant sight of Charles, in a pale green cashmere V-neck that matched his beautiful eyes. 'Delicious wine,' said Hedda, after Flappy had introduced them to Graham and Joan.

'*Si chiama Bardolino Chiaretto Corte Giardini,*' she said in what she believed was perfect Italian. 'The estate where it's produced is on the south side of Lake Garda, which is so beautiful. It's a little fruity, with floral nuances and a crisp finish. Light but tasty, *no*?'

'It hits the spot,' said Kenneth, taking a swig.

'Certainly does,' agreed Charles, his gaze lingering heavily upon Flappy, who was grateful for the vicar's presence, for temptation was easier to resist in the presence of God's emissary.

'Aren't these lovely?' said Joan, pointing at the border.

'*Alcea rosea,*' said Flappy.

89

Hedda laughed. 'Call them what you like, Flappy, they're still hollyhocks.'

Joan's jaw dropped. Kenneth held his breath. The vicar raised his fluffy eyebrows in surprise. But Hedda carried on walking as if she'd said nothing out of the ordinary. 'Those anemones are pretty too,' she continued.

Flappy didn't know what to say. She stared at Hedda, blinking in astonishment that someone had had the temerity to put her down. Just as she was on the point of pursing her lips, a sure sign of her displeasure, Charles smiled at her, a knowing, appreciative smile that held within it the memory of their moment in the pool house, and the situation was defused. Flappy forgot Hedda's comment and smiled back. She forgot the vicar too, God's emissary on earth, and felt with wicked delight a stirring of the beast that Charles had unleashed inside of her, which was very much still roaming free and raring to go again. Her busy mind raced to find ways of getting Charles on his own. It wasn't going to be easy, but now, having taken offence at Hedda's put-down, she was determined to do it. Temptation was there to be surrendered to, surely? Perhaps there was a lesson from God in *that*?

Hedda made such a fuss of Flappy's dinner – her dining room was charming, the table a delight and what pretty hydrangeas, such an unusually dark shade of blue – that Flappy was not able to remain offended by her for long. She introduced each wine in her best Spanish, Italian and French, all of which she had learned by heart, having asked Persephone to write down the phrases for her. Hedda was suitably impressed. 'I'm terrible at languages,' she said. 'I do envy you being able to speak so many.'

'My German is terrible,' said Flappy. 'Don't ask me to say anything in German.'

'Flappy is a woman of many talents,' said Kenneth.

'She clearly is,' agreed the vicar. 'Your culinary skills are second to none. I don't think I've ever tasted a more delicious lasagne.'

'Thank you, Graham,' Flappy replied graciously. 'The secret is in the tomatoes. I go to great lengths to buy tomatoes from the farmers' market because tomatoes in supermarkets can taste of nothing. The reason why Italian food is so *buono* is because the fruit and vegetables are so full of taste. It's the climate, you see. We have to fake it with greenhouses. Not the same. *No?*'

Charles, who was sitting next to Flappy, pressed his leg against hers. Flappy's smile did not waver. If Flappy was good at one thing it was maintaining a poker face in the most challenging of circumstances. 'Is there anything you can't do, Flappy?' he asked.

Flappy laughed a light, tinkling laugh, a *careless* laugh, as he pressed his leg harder against hers. 'Oh, there's plenty I can't do, I'm sure,' she said.

'She just hasn't found it yet,' said Kenneth with a laugh. The vicar and Joan laughed too, for they hadn't either.

Then Hedda gave a little shrug. 'Golf,' she said, and no one could dispute *that*.

After dinner and copious amounts of wine, the group made their way into the drawing room. 'What a charming room,' said Hedda with genuine appreciation. 'You have such a good eye, Flappy.'

'Coming from you, Hedda, that's high praise indeed,' said Flappy happily.

'Oh, I can't take credit for my house. I have a wonderful decorator from London who did it all for me. I'm hopeless at that sort of thing. Just can't be bothered. I'd rather someone else chose the fabrics and furnishings for me.'

'Well, I suppose it's fair to say that I didn't do it *all* by myself. I got a teeny bit of help from Gerald,' said Flappy. 'We work together, Gerald and I, my decorator.'

'You work very well together,' said Joan agreeably.

'We're redecorating a little cottage we have at the bottom of the garden. I used to use it as a painting studio, but I was just so busy I didn't have time to paint. So, I'm going to transform it into a meditation room instead. I do like to meditate,' she said, turning to the vicar. 'In these busy times meditation is imperative for a calm and uncluttered mind, don't you think, Graham?'

'Meditation?' said Hedda, eyes widening with interest.

Flappy's heart stopped. The last thing she needed was Hedda joining her in her little sanctuary and chanting 'Om' beside her. 'Well, yes, but—'

'Charles adores that sort of thing. Tarot cards, gurus and goodness knows what else.' She turned to her husband. 'Meditation is just up your street. Perhaps you and Flappy could do it together?'

Flappy kept her cool. If she was good at one thing it was keeping her cool when coolness was required. Right now, it was required more than ever, because the beast inside of Flappy was rousing and in danger of giving itself away. The image of her and Charles in that lovely big bed beneath the eaves of the cottage floated into her mind and set her pulse racing. 'Do you, Charles?' said Flappy in a mildly disinterested tone.

'I try to meditate every morning, before breakfast, but something always gets in the way of it. It's very frustrating. I don't think meditating at home works for me.'

'Then you must come and use my sanctuary,' said Flappy. 'I will give you a key and you can use it whenever you like.'

'That's very sweet of you, Flappy,' said Charles.

'Oh, it's nothing, really. You can get to it without coming to the house. There's a farm track that runs along the back of our property. We're so *so* lucky to be surrounded by farmland. Not a neighbour for miles. You can park your car there and wander up the path.'

'That sounds ideal,' he added.

'I've asked Persephone, my PA, to find me a guru. You know, someone to teach me how to meditate properly. You see, my mind is so busy, I find it impossible to quieten it.'

'Yes, you need a guru. An Indian guru. Someone who knows what he's doing,' Hedda agreed.

'That would be perfect,' said Flappy.

'You'll be levitating in no time,' said Kenneth with a chuckle. 'The two of you, levitating through the roof!'

Flappy didn't dare catch Charles's eye. She turned to Joan,

because Joan was a safe cove in what was becoming quite a choppy ocean. 'Do *you* meditate, Joan?'

'I don't, but I really should, shouldn't I?'

Then, just in case Joan thought she was going to be invited to Flappy's sanctuary with Charles, Flappy replied, 'No, meditation is not for everyone.'

Flappy was in such a state of excitement she was unable to sleep. All she could think about was she and Charles in that delightfully big bed and all the delicious things he might do to her. She'd given up her guilt, just tossed it away. After all, Hedda had suggested it and Kenneth hadn't so much as turned a hair at the idea of her and Charles meditating together in the cottage. No one minded. An affair hadn't crossed anyone's mind, but hers and Charles's.

The night passed slowly and fretfully. The beast inside of Flappy was restless. Having said she would definitely not do it again, that she would resist temptation, she now accepted that she was already a fallen woman so she might as well stay fallen. After all, there was no point wasting energy struggling against something which could never be overcome. As for getting caught, Charles seemed not to worry about that, so she wouldn't either. Affairs had been going on for as long as humans had been on the earth. Most people never got found out. The few that did were just careless or reckless, or just plain stupid. Flappy was none of those things. She would be careful. If there was one thing Flappy was good at, it was being careful.

The following day dawned cloudy and grey, but Flappy awoke with enthusiasm as if the sun was a giant sunflower in a cornflower-blue sky. It was 5 a.m. She put on her yoga ensemble, which was a pair of pale grey leggings and a white T-shirt, and headed down to the pool house with a spring in her step. In her gym, in front of a vast mirror that took up the entire back wall, Flappy did her stretches and balances to the gentle sound of a flute.

Flappy was good at yoga. She'd practised for years and was as bendy and supple as she'd been twenty years ago. However, no one had seen her naked in a very long time. Even Kenneth, in the last twenty years, hadn't seen her without something covering her body. Flappy was aware that she'd once had a beautiful body. As a young woman she had never appreciated it as she should have. Only now, in late middle age, could she look back and see the loveliness of what she once had and lament its loss. *Youth is wasted on the young*, she thought as she moved smoothly into Warrior I pose. The thought of Charles seeing her without her clothes on was very worrying. In fact, she didn't think she'd worried about anything quite so much as she now worried about that. Even as a newly-wed she had not walked around naked. Walking around naked was very undignified. If there was one thing that Flappy abhorred, it was being undignified.

Charles was going to see her naked. There was no avoiding it. If they were going to make love in the cottage, which she was pretty sure they would, he was going to take her clothes off. Flappy knew she was better with her clothes on. She was very good with her clothes on – in fact, it would be fair to say that she was the best-dressed woman in Badley Compton. She just wasn't as good with her clothes *off*.

She moved seamlessly into Humble Warrior pose. How could she avoid Charles seeing her naked? Of course she could close the curtains. Lighting was very important. Dim lighting was the best. After all, too dark meant fumbling about trying to find things, which would be awkward; too bright and those things, once found, would be much too visible. Dim was definitely the most flattering.

Flappy slipped into Warrior II pose and took a deep breath. If Charles had been making love to Hedda then Flappy really had nothing to worry about. In comparison to the Ayrshire cow, Flappy's white tigress was a damn sight more attractive.

After yoga Flappy showered, changed, spritzed herself with perfume and went downstairs to have breakfast. She poured a few raspberries and a scoop of natural yogurt into a bowl and sat down to read the *Daily Mail*. *'George wasn't that experienced in sex scenes'. Co-star reveals how she got Clooney to 'let go'.* Flappy put a spoonful of yogurt into her mouth and read the story with interest. A little later Kenneth appeared. He found *The Times* on the dining table waiting for him with his cup of coffee. The *Daily Mail* was nowhere to be seen.

'Good morning, darling,' said Flappy, bringing her tea and lemon to the table. 'Can I make you some breakfast?'

'Lovely,' said Kenneth, sitting down and picking up the newspaper. 'A couple of pieces of toast with fried eggs would do the trick.'

'Off to play golf?' she asked, although the question was merely to make conversation. It was apparent from his attire that he was heading to the golf course.

'Yes, with Charles and Algie.'

'Oh, it's Algie now, is it?' said Flappy, delighted he was on 'Algie' terms with Sir Algernon.

'After the game we had, it's Algie all the way.'

'Might Charles be coming to use the pool today?' she asked breezily.

'I don't know. I'll ask him, if you like.'

'Only that I'd like to show him the cottage and give him a key. My sanctuary is not set up yet, but it won't take long and he can start using it now.'

'That's a good idea.'

'Yes, I thought it was. Why don't you tell him to come round this afternoon. I've got a very busy day, but I'm sure I can squeeze him in.'

Once again Kenneth gazed at his wife, his little eyes full of wonder. 'Really, darling, I don't know how you do it.'

'Do what, darling?' she said with a smile.

'Everything. You just manage to do everything.'

Flappy put a hand on his arm. 'You're very sweet to notice.'

'Oh, I do,' he said.

After hoovering up his eggs and toast, he looked at his Rolex. 'Better be off, then. See you for lunch.'

'Have a lovely morning, darling, and don't forget to tell Charles.'

At eleven o'clock Flappy arrived at the church with Persephone to do the flowers. The ladies of Badley Compton took it in turns and this week it was Flappy's. She opened the boot of her Range Rover where the flowers, cut from her own garden by one of her gardeners, lay neatly on a waterproof rug. 'I always feel a teeny bit bad,' she told Persephone as the girl lifted the rug and flowers out of the boot. 'My displays are always far superior to everyone else's. But it can't be helped.' She followed Persephone up the path to the church. 'I'm so *so* lucky to have so many flowers to choose from,' she added, her mind's eye sweeping over the many beautiful gardens at Darnley.

Persephone laid the flowers on the floor in the nave and went back to the car for the vases. Flappy put her hands on her hips and looked around the church. It was so ancient it was mentioned in the Domesday Book. She sat down in her seat, the one Hedda had stolen the previous Sunday, and remembered the first time she had laid eyes on Charles. Really, she still couldn't imagine how Hedda had got him. Perhaps he'd married her for her money, she mused. He couldn't have married her for her looks, and her brain, while being perfectly adequate, hadn't shown signs of being anything out of the ordinary. And Charles was not an ordinary man. No, he most certainly wasn't. He was a cut above. If there was one thing that put terror into Flappy's heart, it was the ordinary. God forbid she ever sank to being *that*.

A few minutes later Persephone appeared with two vases. 'Well done, Persephone,' said Flappy, standing up. 'Hand me the secateurs and I will work my magic.' This she did to great effect. Not only did Flappy have an eagle eye, but she had a good eye when it came to aesthetics too. She knew – better than anyone in Badley Compton, it must be acknowledged – how to arrange flowers. The effect was stunning and even Persephone, who was much too intelligent not to notice Flappy's flaws, had to admit that she had a gift. 'I can see why the other ladies envy your arrangements,' she said. 'It's not just the choice of flowers but the way you put them together.'

'I once did a flower arranging course,' Flappy confessed. 'Many years ago, when I was just married. I thought Kenneth would appreciate a wife who knew how to do that sort of thing.'

'It paid off,' said Persephone.

'It most certainly did,' agreed Flappy, standing back to admire her work. 'It's a lovely church, isn't it. Quaint and full of charm. I don't suppose you're religious, are you? Young people aren't these days.'

'Not really,' Persephone replied. 'Although I want to get married in a church.'

'Yes, the big white wedding. The fairy tale. Girls still grow up wanting that, I suppose.'

'Were your daughters married here?'

'No, Charlotte was married on a beach in Mauritius and Mathilda in Australia. I had nothing to do with either.' Flappy sighed a little sadly. 'I had rather dreamed of Badley Compton weddings for my girls. That's the thing about children, one imagines they're going to be smaller versions of oneself, but they're very much their own people and often remarkably different to their parents. Sometimes, one wonders where they come from. Neither Charlotte nor Mathilda have ever wanted what I want. In fact, I think they have probably gone the other way just to be awkward.' She smiled at Persephone and Persephone saw, for the first time, a glimpse of Honest Flappy. The Flappy without airs. The *Real* Flappy. 'I don't think I was an easy mother,' she said in a quiet voice. 'I've always had impossibly high standards. Hindsight is a wonderful thing. I sometimes wonder, although, I must confess, not very often, might they have settled in England had I done things differently?'

'You'll never know the answer to that, Mrs Scott-Booth, but children always want independent lives from their parents, don't they, so it's not unusual to settle in another country.'

'Do you have a good relationship with your mother, Persephone?'

'Up and down,' she replied with a smile. 'Families are complicated.'

'They are indeed,' said Flappy, smiling back. 'Thank you for your help, Persephone. I don't know what I'd do without you. I'm so *so* lucky to have a PA.'

Chapter 8

That afternoon, Flappy waited in the garden for Charles. Kenneth had returned from golf and told her that Charles was coming to swim at four and would love to be shown the cottage. As wonderful as this news was, it also sent Flappy into a terrible state of panic, fuelled by guilt. It was wrong to use Kenneth as a messenger. It was disrespectful and cruel. Let us be honest, Flappy might have had the odd, tiny flaw – she was not ignorant of her shortcomings – but she was never *ever* disrespectful and cruel. She was aware that, if she was to survive in this new world of extramarital dalliances, she must not lose her moral compass. They would have to find a way of not involving Kenneth.

Charles arrived at five to four and was already lifting his chic leather holdall out of the boot of his Bentley when Flappy wafted round the corner in her trilby and dark glasses, a loose white shirt billowing about her body with the scent of tuberose. 'Charles,' she trilled happily, waving the *Spectator*. 'I was just taking a few minutes out of my busy day to catch up on my favourite magazine.'

Charles kissed her cheek. 'You smell delicious,' he said, inhaling with relish.

Flappy laughed to hide her arousal. After all, Kenneth could appear at any moment, and the gardeners were all over the place, like gnomes toiling away behind every bush. 'Did you have a good game of golf?' she asked.

'Very good. But now I'll have a swim, and then ...' He looked at her intensely, taking in every detail of her beautiful face. 'And then I'll have *you*.'

Flappy's mouth opened and then closed. She was lost for words. The presumption! The nerve! The sheer arrogance of the man. It defied belief and yet, and yet, she had never felt so excited in her life.

'Perhaps you'll show me the cottage,' he continued, holding her steady in his spellbinding gaze.

Flappy felt very hot. She fanned herself with the magazine. After a short internal struggle, she found her voice, husky though it was. 'Of course. Just come and find me when you're done. I'll be in the garden.' She knew that if she accompanied him to the pool house he would kiss her again and then the kiss would lead to something else, and really, they were lucky not to have got caught the first time; she did not want to tempt the Fates. 'Enjoy your swim,' she said.

Charles disappeared into the house and Flappy went round to the terrace where she plonked herself down on one of the reclining chairs and closed her eyes. She sighed heavily. This was total madness, she thought, feeling dangerously out of control. If there was one thing Flappy was very good at, it was being in control. But now that control was slipping through her fingers like sand. All her good intentions had evaporated, leaving the beast within free to wreak havoc. Indeed, the desires of the body were too strong for the mind to harness; she wanted Charles and she wanted him *now*. She didn't think she had ever wanted anything so badly in all her life. She flicked open the magazine and ran her eyes over the words, although she failed to take in their meaning. She closed her eyes again and wondered how long he was going to take doing his lengths.

Fifteen minutes later she heard him call out her name. She sat up with a start. 'Here!' she shouted back. 'In the garden.'

Charles appeared with his hair wet and tousled and Flappy's breath caught in her throat. She got off the chair and put the magazine down. 'Right, let me show you where my shrine is going to be,' she said, making her voice light and carefree. If there was one thing Flappy was good at it was pretending to be one thing when she was really quite another.

They set off through the garden. Flappy did not linger as she normally would, to give her guest time to appreciate the neatly weeded borders, topiary sculptures, ornamental fountains and arches of vines and walkways of roses, no, she strode on with one thing in mind and one thing only: to get to the cottage as quickly as possible to satisfy the urgent demands of her loins.

They arrived at last and, with a trembling hand, Flappy put the key in the lock and turned it. The door opened, releasing the warm and musty smell of an idle house. 'Welcome,' she said and stepped inside.

Charles closed the door behind him and swept his gaze

over the room, settling it finally onto Flappy with its green and hypnotic power. Before Flappy could explain where the statue of Buddha was going to go, or where she might clear space for a small fountain because water was a very soothing sound for meditators, his lips were upon hers and his arms were around her body, and he was kissing her deeply and passionately and awakening the beast inside her with a jolt. Her legs gave way, she fell against him like a rag doll, powerless to resist the force of his magnetism. She was truly lost and loving every moment of it, and thinking that, if she never found herself again, she'd be completely content.

Then Flappy remembered the high bed beneath the eves. She took his hand out from under her shirt and led him upstairs. Without a word they fell onto the soft mattress. Flappy would have liked to have had time to close the curtains. Now Charles was going to see her naked body in bright sunshine, for the sun was indeed shining in through the window. She shut her eyes. It couldn't be helped and, as he buried his face in her neck and ran his hands over the skin beneath her shirt, she decided that she really didn't care. He was used to making love to an Ayrshire cow, after all. A white tigress would be a dramatic improvement.

After Charles had brought Flappy to unimagined heights of pleasure, they lay entwined beneath the sheets, pink-cheeked and sparkly eyed and out of breath, for, at their age, that kind of lovemaking was something of a marathon. 'That was wonderful,' Flappy breathed, believing that she had never experienced anything quite so wonderful in her entire life.

'You're a beautiful woman, Flappy,' he replied. 'I've been dreaming of this moment ever since you mentioned this secret little sanctuary, and it didn't disappoint. You're a goddess. Much too good for me.'

'Oh, Charles. That's just silly.' But Flappy knew why he should think such a thing. She was, it was true, much too good for most men. 'You're a cut above all the others,' she said. 'We're perfect for each other.'

'How fortunate that we chose to come and live in Badley Compton,' he said.

'Well, it is a charming place and more cultured than one would expect—'

'No, I mean because of *you*, Flappy. I'm fortunate to have found *you*.'

Flappy smiled with pleasure. 'That's a very nice thing to say.'

'Do you make love with Kenneth?' he asked suddenly, an undercurrent of jealousy in his tone.

Flappy wasn't sure how to respond. She didn't want to say anything that might diminish her in his eyes and she did not want to be more disloyal to Kenneth than she was already being. 'Let's not talk about Kenneth and Hedda,' she said. 'Let it just be you and me, Charles. Here in this parallel world. In this little sanctuary of pleasure.'

'You're so right, Flappy,' he agreed. 'I should not have asked. Forgive me.'

She snuggled into his chest. 'Of course, my darling. I'll forgive you anything.'

Flappy and Charles agreed that, in future, although both Hedda and Kenneth were aware that Charles was going to use the cottage for meditation, they would be discreet. They'd meet in the cottage around five, arriving separately with a ten-minute gap. Charles would park his car on the farm track behind the property and Flappy would trot through the gardens. It would be perfect, cautious and, Flappy was certain, foolproof. No one came to the cottage, ever. Kenneth hadn't been there since Flappy had given the town a small exhibition of her paintings, raising money for much needed repairs to the town hall, in the process of which she had easily exceeded the required amount by selling out. Indeed, there were many of her watercolours hanging on the walls of the great and the good of Badley Compton.

As they walked back up through the gardens towards the house, Flappy asked Charles about his acting career. 'I gather you were an actor,' she said, stopping to smell a late-flowering rose.

'Yes, I was,' he replied and Flappy felt a frisson of pleasure. She pictured him in on skis, jumping off a precipice and releasing a wonderfully patriotic Union Jack parachute.

'Do you remember *Fawlty Towers*?' he said.

'Oh yes, John Cleese. Of course I remember that!' said Flappy excitedly.

'I did a screen test for one of the hotel guests.'

'Did you?'

'Yes, but I didn't get it. I was so close,' he said, showing her just how close he was with his forefinger and thumb.

'Oh, bad luck, darling,' she cooed. 'What else?'

'I also auditioned for *Withnail and I*.'

'That was a brilliant film,' said Flappy, impressed. She narrowed her eyes, trying to work out which part he could have played, for surely, besides Withnail, Marwood, Uncle Monty and Danny, there weren't very many to choose from – he certainly wasn't the grumpy old farmer.

'I was going to play Isaac Parkin, but I was struck down with glandular fever and had to pull out.'

'That's a shame,' said Flappy in disappointment.

'But I did the odd advert when I wasn't committed.'

Flappy's heart sank. Surely not Daks!

'Daz washing powder,' he said and laughed. 'Oh, the things I did when I was young and naive.'

Flappy did not want to dwell anymore on his acting career, if one could even call it that, which one couldn't, not really. 'What did you do when you stopped being an actor?' she asked, hoping for something a teeny bit more glamorous.

'I retired,' he said.

'Oh,' said Flappy.

'I've been retired for a very long time.' By that he must surely mean about forty years. 'But like you, Flappy, I fill my days with interesting things. My main hobby is collecting art.'

'Of course,' Flappy exclaimed with relief. That's just what a gentleman like Charles Harvey-Smith would do, collect great works of art. 'Much more dignified than acting,' she added.

'Much,' Charles agreed. 'Do you like Hockney?'

'Of course!' she cried. 'Who doesn't like Hockney!'

'Well, I've got my eye on one of those.'

The following morning it was pouring with rain. Flappy lay in bed listening to the rattling sound of raindrops against her windowpanes and felt very content. She stretched out luxuriously and smiled to herself as the memory of the afternoon before came back to her in delicious waves of erotic pleasure. Never had her body felt so loose. Never had she felt so supple. Never *ever* had she felt so alive. Flappy, queen of Badley Compton, was living a double life! Who'd have thought it?

It being a Saturday, Persephone would not be coming in. Nor would the gardeners. Nor would Karen and nor would Tatiana who came every morning to clean. Kenneth would have to cancel his golf, which was a shame, because otherwise she would have had the house to herself. She looked at the clock on her bedside table. It was seven. Flappy always awoke at five. This was extraordinary. Quite extraordinary. She sat up with a start.

She slipped on her yoga clothes and made her way down to the pool. She stood a moment, gazing into the shimmering water. She imagined Charles gliding through it in his swimming trunks and a ripple of desire careered over her skin, making her feel suddenly reckless. If there was one thing Flappy *never* felt, it was reckless. Without a moment's hesitation she took off her clothes, *all* of them. Then she dived into the pool, a perfect dive, because, it must be acknowledged, Flappy was a beautiful swimmer. She promptly swam a length of front crawl, followed by an elegant breaststroke, followed by backstroke. The sensation of the cool water against her naked body, reaching into every nook and cranny, made her feel wickedly sensual. She did not feel like a woman in her sixties, but a young woman in the first throes of love. A beautiful, flawless young woman with boundless energy and desire. Yes, desire! Who'd have thought it?

Flappy was a new woman. Instead of yoga, she put on some pop music – she secretly loved Kylie Minogue – and danced naked in front of the mirror. The joy that bubbled inside her was uncontainable. Out it spilled in hip-wiggles and sways, jumps and bounces. By the end of the song she was out of breath and laughing wildly. Her hair had dried into a mop of frizz and her eyes were ablaze with passion. Passion for life, passion for Charles and passion for the bold new Flappy who was grinning, a little madly it must be said, out at her from the mirror.

When Kenneth awoke in the big bed in his dressing room, he heard singing. He lay there a moment wondering whether Flappy had turned on the radio in her bedroom. It was very unlike Flappy to play anything other than classical music. If there was one thing he knew Flappy abhorred, it was pop music. But no, as he sat up in bed, his belly making it quite impossible to stay up without falling back against the pillows, he realized with surprise that it was indeed pop music and, as he cocked an ear, that the voice belonged to Flappy.

'*I can't get you out of my head,*' sang Flappy happily as she applied make-up at her vanity table in her bedroom next door. '*La la la la la . . .*' Kenneth blinked hard. Perhaps he was dreaming. Flappy never sang, except in church – as one would expect, she had an angelic voice. But no, he wasn't dreaming. He climbed out of bed with a groan and took a moment to steady himself as he was suddenly assaulted by a head-spin. He wandered into the bathroom and peed. Then he brushed his teeth. All the while his wife sang loudly and confidently in the room next door. Finally, her voice was drowned out by the hairdryer. Kenneth hated loud noises, so he went back into his dressing room and opened the curtains. When he saw the rain he was disappointed. There would be no golf today. He sighed and looked up at the sky, hoping that a patch of blue would appear in the cloud. It did not. He stared some more, just in case. But no, still low hanging clouds the colour of porridge. He went to his cupboard and pulled out a pair of red chinos, a white polo shirt and a yellow cashmere V-neck. The sort of clothes he wore when he wasn't going to play golf. Disappointed clothes.

When the hairdryer stopped he went in to see his wife. 'Good morning, darling,' she said when she saw him.

Kenneth blinked twice then narrowed his eyes. He couldn't put his finger on what, but there was something decidedly different about her today. The hair was the same, her face was the same and she was wearing a typically chic ensemble that she would claim she had just 'thrown on' without any thought, but still, there was something *different* and a little alarming. But, because he couldn't identify it, he couldn't mention it either. 'You're in a good mood today, darling,' was all he said.

'I am. It's Saturday. I love Saturdays. No one in the house but us.'

'Well, yes, I suppose that's true. But I thought you loved

it when the place was teeming with people, making it all nice for you.'

'Oh, I do, of course. I never *ever* take that for granted. I'm so *so* lucky to have countless people tending to Darnley. But today, I'm actually loving the fact that we're alone.'

'Right, well, shall we have some breakfast?'

'Yes, breakfast. I'm ravenous.' Flappy led the way downstairs and into the kitchen. Kenneth was feeling uneasy. Flappy singing? Flappy wanting to be alone? Then, horror of horrors, Flappy buttering a thick slice of toast and dipping 'soldiers' into her boiled egg. 'I haven't done this since I was a child,' she laughed. 'Isn't this fun!'

Kenneth frowned over his coffee cup. 'I don't think you've eaten bread in all the years we've been married,' he said, smiling to mask his anxiety.

'I'm going to have milk in my tea,' she said, lifting the bottle out of the fridge and bringing it to the table. She did not, as she usually did, pour milk into a jug, no, she poured it straight from the bottle into her teacup. 'Don't look so surprised, Kenneth. I awoke this morning feeling different.'

Kenneth's shoulders relaxed. At least Flappy had noticed too, he thought. What a relief! 'I was going to comment on it, but I wasn't sure what it was,' he said.

'I awoke feeling happy, darling. Very, very happy. For a start, I awoke at seven.'

'Seven?'

'I know, isn't that extraordinary. Quite extraordinary. And then I went downstairs to do yoga, but decided to go for a swim instead.'

111

'A swim?' gasped Kenneth, putting down his coffee cup in case he dropped it. Flappy would not want him to break her pretty pastel-coloured set from Fortnum's in London.

'Yes, a swim! I haven't swum in about forty years. And then—'

'There's more?' he interrupted.

'I danced.'

'You danced?'

'Yes, I danced instead of yoga.' She did not go as far as telling him that she had danced *naked*. That would be too much information for her poor husband to take in. As it was his face had gone pale and he was looking fearful. She put a hand on his. 'Darling, don't look so worried. I'm not sick. I'm just happy!'

'But why are you so happy?' he asked.

Now Flappy had to choose her words carefully. Very carefully. She did not want to give her husband any reason to suspect foul play. 'I'm so *so* lucky, darling,' she said, looking at him with tenderness. 'I have everything I want. Everything. In fact, there is nothing I want that I don't have. And it's all because of *you*.' Kenneth frowned again, still looking fearful. 'I think I awoke with an enormous sense of gratitude, darling. It just came over me all of a sudden and filled me with joy. One mustn't be so spoilt as to take all one's blessings for granted. Especially when one has so *many* blessings. Don't you agree?'

Kenneth was moved. He didn't know what to say. He squeezed his wife's hands and gave her a grateful smile.

The following day Flappy and Kenneth went to church at the normal time. Flappy did not insist they go early. In fact, they arrived a minute or two late. Everyone was already seated and, as Flappy walked down the aisle, she smiled serenely at the faces turned towards her. However, she had eyes for one person and one person only: Charles. Flappy noticed at once that the Harvey-Smiths had put themselves in the front row of the other side of the church and were looking perfectly content about it. Hedda gave her a little wave and Flappy waved back. Charles caught her eye but Flappy looked away; it was imperative that she control herself in public, when the eyes of the entire congregation were upon her.

She sat down in her place and took a moment to thank God for her blessings in a quiet prayer. Right now she really did have a lot to thank Him for, and a little to apologize for, too, she had to admit. But God was notoriously forgiving, she reasoned, as she cut off her conversation and opened her prayer book. She was one of His sheep who was currently straying from His ways. If she remembered rightly, God loved those kind of sheep the most.

Chapter 9

After a pleasant but not very inspiring Sunday lunch at Mabel and John Hitchens' house, Flappy and Kenneth headed home in Kenneth's sleek Jaguar. 'I'm not going to wait for Gerald to decorate the cottage,' she told him. 'I'm going to start meditating right away. There's no time like the present, is there, when one has come up with a good project?'

'Quite,' Kenneth replied, slowing down behind a lorry. He pulled out a little to see if he could overtake, then swerved back into his lane again when he discovered that he couldn't.

'I mean, one is very enthusiastic to get started, in the beginning.'

'Then you lose interest,' said Kenneth.

'If you're referring to my painting, Kenneth, I didn't lose interest. I was just too busy to keep it going. For painting, one requires time. Hours, in fact, of peace and solitude. With meditation, one requires an hour and then it's done. Of course, if one has gone very deep into oneself, then perhaps one requires a teeny bit more than an hour,' she added, thinking of Charles and the likelihood of that hour slipping into two. 'After all, the idea is to lose oneself completely. I'm going to start this afternoon and I don't want to be disturbed. If you need me, you must telephone. Is that all right, darling? Only, if you were to appear at the door when I was in mid-flow, you might startle me, and perhaps even kill me. I mean, it might be like waking someone up while they're dreaming.'

'I think that's an old wives' tale,' said Kenneth.

'I don't want to discover that it isn't,' said Flappy. 'So, the cottage is my sanctuary, my little place of peace and solitude, where I can commune with my Higher Self, without interruption.'

Kenneth wasn't sure what her Higher Self was. But he didn't think Flappy had one, being so 'high' already. However, he agreed not to disturb her when she was there, then, taking the opportunity of a clear road, he overtook the lorry with a roar.

Flappy and Charles had devised a way of communicating secretly with a double blink. A *double* blink meant five o'clock at the cottage – a long *single* blink meant the rendezvous could not be met. Charles had given her the double blink outside church that morning. Flappy was very excited.

At five minutes to five, Flappy skipped lightly through the gardens, stopping only to pick a rose so she could arrive with it pressed against her nose. She didn't want to look as if she had raced to their meeting without appreciating the gardens and the lovely day, for indeed it was impossible not to appreciate the gardens at Darnley in the sunshine.

Charles had parked his car on the track behind the property and made his way to the cottage as arranged. Having been given a key he had let himself in. When Flappy stepped inside, she found him upstairs, lying on the bed in nothing but his boxer shorts. He patted the place beside him and smiled his most dazzling smile. 'Come to me, Flappy,' he said, and Flappy did, sinking into his arms with the enthusiasm of a young lover and enveloping him in a cloud of tuberose.

The following morning after a swim and a naked dance in front of the mirror to the rousing music of Shania Twain, Flappy joined Kenneth for breakfast. Again he noticed that something was different about her and again he couldn't quite put his finger on what it was. 'Who are you playing golf with today?' she asked cheerfully, because Flappy felt indecently cheerful this morning.

'Charles and Hedda,' he replied.

'Hedda?' said Flappy in surprise, suspending the butter knife over her piece of toast. 'I thought she said she rarely played.'

'Then this must be one of those rare times,' said Kenneth.

Flappy narrowed her eyes, her quick mind working out the reason why Hedda should want to accompany her husband to the golf course. Did she suspect something? Was she keen to keep her husband in her sights? Surely Hedda was not playing golf because she wanted to hit a ball, she was playing golf because she wanted to keep an eye on her husband.

Well, if Kenneth had looked like Charles, Flappy might have wanted to keep an eye on him too!

Flappy hoped Hedda wouldn't decide to join their meditation sessions in the cottage.

Had it not been for the busy day ahead, Flappy might have gone to the golf course with Kenneth. In the early days of their marriage she had often accompanied him, joining him for a stodgy English lunch in the clubhouse after a morning traipsing around after him, being bored. Flappy found the game intolerably dull and his friends intolerable too. Now, however, the game held more appeal because of Charles, and the prospect of Hedda making an unexpected appearance on the course had certainly piqued her interest. But busy days were busy days and Flappy never *ever* cancelled unless sick or responding to a greater need. Golf did not qualify for either. 'Well, I hope you have a lovely day,' she said as Kenneth glanced at his Rolex and decided it was time to head off.

Flappy met Persephone in the hall at nine. 'Good morning, Persephone,' she trilled and Persephone noticed at once the bounce in Flappy's step and the extra width in her smile. Flappy was glowing. In fact, Flappy was giving a whole new meaning to the word 'glow'.

'How was your weekend, Mrs Scott-Booth?' Persephone asked, following her into the library.

'Very jolly, thank you, Persephone,' said Flappy. 'How was yours?'

'Quiet,' Persephone replied.

'You need a nice boyfriend to entertain you,' said Flappy,

and there was something in her smile that told Persephone that Flappy knew what she was talking about.

'A boyfriend would be nice,' said Persephone.

'There is nothing more invigorating than being in love, Persephone. It keeps one young, gives one a delicious endorphin rush, gets the blood pumping around one's body and puts one in an exceedingly good mood.' Persephone knew Flappy was talking about herself. Flappy was unable to refrain from boasting when she had something truly exciting to boast about.

'I haven't met anyone who makes me feel like that,' said Persephone, watching Flappy closely. 'Did Mr Scott-Booth make you feel all of those things?'

'I suppose he must have done once,' said Flappy vaguely, for it was true, they had met so long ago she could barely remember anything about it, and she was realistic enough to know that had Kenneth not made the blood pump around her body at all she would not have married him. 'One never forgets the feeling,' she continued, turning her thoughts once again to Charles. 'It's intoxicating. Delightful. Probably the most heavenly feeling ever.' She sighed. 'Oh, to be young again.' Then she smiled at Persephone. 'You're young. Don't waste it. Appreciate how lovely you are while you're lovely.'

'But you're still beautiful, Mrs Scott-Booth,' said Persephone truthfully.

Persephone was right, of course. Flappy *was* still beautiful. But time was what it was and nothing could stop the gradual corrosion brought about by its relentless tread. 'I know, I haven't lost it yet,' she said with a sniff. 'But I'm teetering on the edge, Persephone. Teetering on the edge.'

Persephone laughed. 'If you knew how people see you, you wouldn't say that,' she said.

'How do people see me?' Flappy asked, eager for the compliment she knew was coming.

'They say you have the secret to eternal youth.'

Flappy had heard that before. However, now was the moment for a self-deprecating remark. If Flappy was good at one thing, it was knowing when not to look smug. 'My secret to eternal youth, Persephone, is an old and ugly portrait in the attic,' she said, referring to the famous story, *The Picture of Dorian Gray* by Oscar Wilde, which she had never read. Flappy did enjoy dropping in the odd literary reference every now and then.

Flappy left Persephone with all the boring things she would usually have done herself – or passed on to one of her ladies-in-waiting, like Mabel – and left for town in her shiny grey Range Rover. She had a parish meeting at eleven, in the town hall, which gave her time for a cup of coffee at Café Délice. Flappy rarely set foot in Big Mary's café. She certainly never went in there with the intention of staying and drinking coffee. That was frightfully common, sipping coffee in a café with the hoi polloi. Yet, for some reason, she felt differently today. She was in a tremendously good mood and rather craved one of Big Mary's sticky buns. What had she called them? Devil's Desire? Her mouth watered at the thought of them as she drove down the leafy lanes in the sunshine, in her dark glasses and trilby, singing along to Celine Dion.

Badley Compton was busy for a Monday morning. Seagulls squabbled about the bins, fishermen tended their boats and ordinary people who were not lucky enough to have a PA hurried down the pavements to the post office, the newsagent or the supermarket. Flappy was unable to find a parking space close to the café, so had to park at the top of the hill beneath some trees and hope that the birds in residence there would not drop unsightly things onto her car. As she wandered down the street she noticed an old man sitting on the bench that she and Kenneth had generously given the town in memory of Harry Pratt, who'd liked to sit and watch the coming and going of little boats in the harbour below. How charming it was, that bench, and how lovely that someone was enjoying it, thought Flappy. She wondered whether he'd read the inscription on the plaque: *In loving memory of Harry Pratt 1919–2010, kindly given to Badley Compton by Kenneth and Flappy Scott-Booth*. It was, indeed, very kindly given, Flappy mused as she crossed the road and headed towards the café, distinguished by the pink-and-white-striped awning and the few tables and chairs arranged on the pavement beneath it.

She pushed open the door. As she'd expected, the café was quite full. It was, after all, the heart of the town. Now Flappy had turned up she suspected it would beat a little faster than usual. She swept her eyes over the faces turning to see who was coming in and spotted John Hitchens at a table with his little granddaughter, their golden retriever lying on the floor at their feet. Esther, Madge and Sally were seated at another, and various other people Flappy knew well enough to greet with a smile and a nod were dotted about the room.

'Hello, Flappy,' said Esther, Madge and Sally in unison. The three of them invited her to join their table. An invitation they assumed would not be accepted because it was well known that Flappy only ever came into the café if she needed to ask Big Mary to cater at one of her events.

'I don't mind if I do,' Flappy replied to the astonishment of the ladies. 'Back in a sec. Good morning, John,' she said, stopping beside his table. 'And who might you be?' she asked his little granddaughter.

'Mattie,' the girl replied.

'Ah yes, Mattie. I've heard a lot about you. You're the one who makes necklaces out of shells, aren't you?' Mattie giggled and nodded. 'How clever you are. I bet they're a lot nicer than anything one can buy in a shop.' She smiled and the child smiled back and Flappy felt an ache in the centre of her chest that surprised her. She was a grandmother, after all, but only got to see her grandchildren once or twice a year. She lifted her chin and sighed. Such was life, she thought, not allowing negative thoughts to dampen her day. If Flappy was good at one thing it was being positive in the face of sorrow. 'Shouldn't you be at school?' she added.

'I'm sick,' said the child.

Flappy laughed because she didn't look sick at all. 'I see. Poor you. Let me buy you a cake. Is that all right, John, if I buy Mattie a cake?'

John looked at his granddaughter with affection. 'Why

don't you go up and choose one with Mrs Scott-Booth.' The child took Flappy's hand.

'You can call me Flappy,' said Flappy, approaching the counter.

'Why are you called Flappy?'

'That's a very good question,' said Flappy, but she didn't answer it. 'Ah, look at all these delicious cakes. Good morning, Mary.'

Big Mary, who was in her usual position behind the counter, greeted Flappy warily. She wasn't used to this new Flappy who was lingering in her café, being sociable. The child chose a cake with sprinkles on it and Flappy chose a Devil's Desire for herself. 'I'll have a cup of coffee too,' she added. 'In for a penny, in for a pound.' She chuckled. Big Mary frowned. She wasn't used to Flappy chuckling either. This was very odd. There was something remarkably different about Flappy today.

'I'll bring everything to the table, Mrs Scott-Booth,' said Big Mary, taking down a mug from the shelf.

Flappy took the child back to her chair, then sat down with her three friends, who had been whispering behind her back, wondering at the change that had come over her. Indeed, she was quite altered. Each of them recalled the change that had come over Gracie Burton when she'd decided, quite suddenly and most uncharacteristically, to go to Italy to do a cookery course. Flappy had vociferously vented her disapproval. If there was one thing she abhorred, she'd said, it was when people ceased to be themselves. What, the three women asked themselves, had come over Flappy?

'Isn't this nice!' Flappy exclaimed, taking off her sunglasses and hooking them in the V of her white linen shirt. 'We should do this more often. What a nice café this is. So full of life.'

'We come here all the time,' said Madge.

Sally laughed to hide her nervousness – it wasn't often that she socialized with Flappy without a drink to give her courage. 'Almost every day, in fact,' she added. 'You're welcome to join whenever you like.'

'Thank you, Sally,' said Flappy. 'What a nice blouse you're wearing,' she added, dropping her eyes to the blue and silver glittery number that Flappy would normally have disliked. If there was one thing she really hated it was glitter.

'Oh, really? I didn't think—' Sally began. She was about to say that she didn't think she'd be bumping into Flappy, otherwise she would have chosen something more suitable. But Flappy cut her off.

'It's delightful. What's not to love about a little cheer? It's uplifting. There's enough negativity in the world, why not put a smile on everyone's face with a bit of dazzle.'

Esther narrowed her eyes. 'You're in a very good mood this morning, Flappy. What's going on?'

'You look wonderful,' Madge added truthfully. For it could not be denied, Flappy was aglow with something new and different and they longed to know what it was.

'*Do* I look wonderful?' she asked in delight, a secretive smile spreading across her face.

'You look like that cat that's got the cream,' said Esther, who was the only one who had the confidence to be so outspoken.

123

'I have taken up meditation,' she announced as if she were the first to have thought of it.

'Meditation?' said Sally. 'Meditation is making you look like *that*?'

'Yes, I'm redecorating my little cottage and turning it into a sanctuary. Gerald is helping me.'

'Have you found a guru to teach you?' asked Madge. She didn't imagine meditation alone had caused such a marked transformation in Flappy.

'Not yet. Persephone is on the case. In the meantime, I am meditating on my own. Every evening at five. It's very peaceful in there. Peaceful and calm and ... ' She sighed, thinking of Charles. 'Heavenly.'

Big Mary brought over Flappy's cup of coffee and cake. Flappy took a bite and shivered with pleasure. 'This is the best cake I have ever tasted,' she said, inhaling through dilated nostrils and closing her eyes to savour it.

Big Mary exchanged glances with the other women. If meditation was having this effect on Flappy, they should all be doing it.

Flappy was in a cheerful mood when she arrived at the town hall for the parish meeting. However, twice she lost her train of thought and twice she had to apologize. 'I've got a lot on my mind right now,' she explained and left the decisions to be made by the other members. It was very unlike Flappy to take a back seat when she was used to driving. But the other women, especially, were grateful to have the opportunity to shine and looked upon the unusually subdued Flappy with an odd combination of appreciation and bewilderment.

At lunch Kenneth told Flappy what an excellent golfer Hedda was. 'She might even be scratch, I tell you. Quite unbelievable. Put us all in the shade,' he said, tucking into Coronation Chicken.

Flappy would normally have been put out by this piece of information. She did not like it when other women excelled beyond her own abilities. But today she felt nothing but joy and admiration for Hedda. 'How clever of her to have such a talent,' she gushed. 'I always admire people with talent, don't I, Kenneth?'

'You certainly do, Flappy,' he replied.

'She's a remarkable woman, isn't she? So gifted and yet so modest about it. I do loathe people who swank and Hedda is not a swanker. I never *ever* boast about my talents and achievements. Much better that people hear about them from others. By swanking, one only sets oneself up for a fall.' She inhaled through her nostrils, satisfied that she was being generous and kind about Charles's wife and feeling very good about herself because of it. 'How is Charles?' she asked breezily. 'Take me through the morning, shot by shot.'

Kenneth assumed that Flappy's interest in the game had more to do with her new friend Hedda than in the golf itself, but he gave her the highlights, relishing the way she gazed at him intensely, listening to his every word. Normally, when he talked about golf, her eyes glazed over and she changed the subject at the first opportunity.

'How fascinating,' said Flappy when he had finished.

'Sometimes I wish I'd had the time to take up golf, you know, when we were young. It would have been something we could have enjoyed together like Hedda and Charles.'

'I don't think Hedda had played for a while. She did say she was rusty.'

'But she wasn't, was she?'

'No, she wasn't.'

'Still,' she said, putting her hand on his. 'We're very happy, aren't we, darling?'

'Very,' he said, smiling at her. 'It makes no difference to me whether you play golf or not.'

'How sweet you are,' she exclaimed, aware that she was meeting Charles at five and feeling a teeny bit guilty about it. Being extra nice to Kenneth made her feel better.

'What are you doing this afternoon?' he asked, putting his napkin on the table for the meal was now over.

'Gerald is bringing my Buddha over at three and then I'm going to meditate at five, which is my usual slot. You do remember, don't you, Kenneth?'

'I won't disturb you,' he reassured her. 'You're so busy giving yourself to everyone, it's right that you should take an hour or so for yourself.'

'Perhaps a teeny bit more than an hour,' said Flappy.

'Take as long as you want,' said Kenneth.

'And then I have the book club,' she added, remembering suddenly that she was meant to have read the book. Not to worry, she thought as she got up from the table, she'd get Persephone to write a brief storyline and a few clever observations about the characters and plot.

At three Gerald appeared with the Buddha, concealed in a cardboard box. Because it was too big to carry, Flappy summoned one of the gardeners who took it down to the cottage in a wheelbarrow. 'How exciting!' Flappy gushed, following behind with Gerald. 'I can't wait to see him. I bet he's beautiful.'

'He is,' said Gerald. 'I'm very pleased with him and I know you will be too.'

'One must have a focal point, mustn't one,' said Flappy, picking the head off a lavender and crunching it between her finger and thumb. 'Ah, what a delicious scent.' She inhaled it loudly. 'We must make sure the room smells lovely too, Gerald. My sense of smell is very acute, as you know.'

'I've already thought of that,' said Gerald, pleased to have pre-empted her. 'I've brought incense from the Buddhist temples in Nepal. I want your sanctuary to be as authentic as possible.'

'You know me so well,' said Flappy with a contented sigh, linking her arm with his.

Once in the cottage, Gerald used a kitchen knife to open the box. He delved into the polystyrene packaging and lifted out a jade Buddha. Flappy gasped. It was just what she'd wanted. 'Darling Gerald, where did you find such a gem?' she asked, watching him place it carefully on the table.

'This fellow comes all the way from Vietnam.'

'Vietnam!' She ran her fingers over the curve of his belly and the folds of his robe. 'He's darling. How clever of you to find him for me. From Vietnam to this sleepy cottage in the middle of Devon. Who'd have thought it?'

'I'm going to build you a shrine over here,' said Gerald, striding purposefully to the other end of the room. 'It's going to be tasteful. I've brought candles and incense. I suggest we place the Buddha in the centre, among ferns, lots of ferns. You need plants to inspire you, Flappy, and I think we should paint the walls a soothing pale green.'

'Wonderful,' said Flappy, clapping her hands in delight, because she was unable to contain this joy that was wanting to burst out of her. 'It's going to be perfect, just perfect.' Then she turned to Gerald and smiled broadly. 'I'm so *so* lucky to have you to do it all for me.'

Chapter 10

Flappy lay in Charles's arms in the big bed beneath the eaves and sighed contentedly. 'Darling Beastie,' she said, for Beastie was the nickname she had given him. 'You are the most wonderful lover. You really are. You make me feel like a teenager.'

'You're a teenager in all but number, Beauty,' he replied, for Beauty was the nickname *he'd* given *her*. 'If you hadn't told me how old you are, I would have guessed you were at least twenty years younger. I don't know how you do it.'

'There's a portrait of me in the attic which is growing old and ugly,' she laughed, repeating smoothly the line she'd used a dozen times.

'I doubt that very much. You will grow old, as we all will, but you will never grow ugly.' Flappy was inclined to believe him, although growing old was bad enough. 'I like our *cinque à sept,* the lovers' hours. It makes me feel like I'm in Paris in the eighteenth century. I think everyone should have a lover. It puts one in such a good mood. I'm nicer to Kenneth, for example. Actually, I'm in such a good mood I'm nicer to everyone. Do you know, today, at the parish meeting, my mind drifted off twice and I had to make something up. I couldn't say I was dreaming about my lover and all the delicious things he was going to do to me at five o'clock.' She laughed throatily.

Charles rolled onto his side and growled (like a beast). 'I think I'm ready to do all those deliciously wicked things to you again,' he said, taking her wrists and pinning them above her head. 'Are you ready for another round, Beauty?'

By the time Mabel, Esther, Madge and Sally arrived at Darnley for the book club meeting Flappy had already drunk two glasses of prosecco (while singing along to Cliff Richard in the bath) and was lounging on the sofa in the drawing room in a long pleated skirt and pearl-grey cashmere sweater, with her third in her hand. There was something loose and uncharacteristically casual about her look. It wasn't very Flappy. Quite apart from the clothes, she was not wearing any jewellery and her hair was slightly tousled. This new, unpredictable Flappy made the four women feel extremely uneasy. Something was afoot. Could it really be the meditation?

'Help yourselves,' Flappy instructed from the sofa. 'There's prosecco *molto freddo e delizioso*, and a bottle of *vino bianco*, if anyone would prefer that. I want you all to be happy. *Tutte molto felici!*' They poured their drinks in stunned silence as Flappy held forth with a half-empty crystal flute. 'Gerald came round today with a Buddha. It's made of jade and is absolutely the most beautiful Buddha I've ever seen. You see, if one is going to make a sanctuary one has to do it properly, or it's not worth doing at all. Gerald knows that. Gerald knows me so well. I'm so *so* lucky to have Gerald.'

Sally and Madge took their drinks to the sofa, Esther and Mabel took theirs to the armchairs. They all sat down. Suddenly, into Flappy's busy mind popped an idea. She pushed herself up with purpose. 'Come, let me show you my Buddha. You must see him. You can't really appreciate how delightful he is without seeing him for yourselves.'

The four women got up. 'Bring your drinks,' Flappy added, wafting over to the drinks tray to refill her glass. 'One mustn't let one's glass get too low,' she said with a giggle, filling it almost to the top.

'Flappy, are you all right?' asked Mabel, panicking suddenly that Flappy might be having a breakdown. Didn't people go mad sometimes before they had a breakdown?

'Mabel darling, I have never been better. Never. I'm *molto felice. Molto, molto felice.*' She waved at them as she marched through the French doors. 'Come, come. Before it gets dark and we all fall into the rose bushes.'

The five of them set off through the gardens, the *many beautiful* gardens, which were cultivated so devotedly at Darnley. The sun was setting, turning the sky a pale orange-pink, and birds twittered in the branches of the horse chestnut trees, settling down to roost and making quite a fuss about it. Dew was already dampening the grass as the shadows lengthened and the air grew cold. Autumn was edging in slowly, eating away the last of the summer days.

Flappy was buoyant. She walked with a skip in her step, stopping every now and then to smell a flower and comment on it. The four women hurried along behind her, exchanging anxious glances. It was a very strange thing to see Flappy like this. Was she perhaps in a state of bliss? they wondered. Was this what Buddha had meant when he talked about Enlightenment? Had Flappy reached Nirvana? Could Nirvana be reached in only a week?

They arrived at the cottage and Flappy put the key in the lock and turned it. She inhaled the smell of incense, for when she and Charles had been there earlier that evening she had shown him her Buddha and lit a stick of incense, filling the cottage with the smell of a Nepalese temple. She inhaled deeply. 'Isn't it divine!' she said, referring to the scent. 'It lifts one, doesn't it? Makes one feel quite giddy.'

Sally looked around the room. She had never been into Flappy's cottage before. It would be the perfect place to write, she thought, nestled in the trees right at the bottom of the garden, in tranquillity and solitude. 'It's gorgeous!' she exclaimed enviously. 'What a jewel.'

Flappy floated over to the Buddha, which Gerald had placed in situ against the wall with the incense and tea lights. 'He's come all the way from Vietnam,' she told them, caressing him fondly.

'So, what do you do?' asked Esther, trying to picture Flappy cross-legged on the carpet going 'Om'.

'I sit here,' Flappy replied, imagining what she would

do were she to meditate, which she hadn't yet because of Charles. 'And I put my hands like this.' She demonstrated, resting her thumbs against her fingers. 'Then I focus on my breathing. In through the nose, out through the mouth. With every outward breath, I go deeper and deeper until I am far, far away. I am a nothing. I am beyond ego. Beyond the cares of life. I am at one with the Source.'

'The Source?' asked Esther, screwing up her nose. It all sounded a bit too New Agey for her liking.

'The Source is what you'd call God,' Madge answered, taking a swig of prosecco. 'It's the Light. Where we all come from.'

'And where we are all going,' Flappy added, a beatific smile on her face, which suggested she was a teeny bit further along the path than they were.

'Can anyone do it?' asked Mabel, because if it really was meditation that was making Flappy so relaxed and happy, then she'd like to do it too.

'Of course anyone can do it,' Flappy answered. 'We all have to start somewhere. One gets better with practice.'

'Why don't we start a meditation club, like our book club?' suggested Mabel. 'You could teach us how to do it, Flappy.'

Flappy did not look as excited about it as Mabel expected. 'Well . . . ' she began, crinkling her nose.

'What a brilliant idea!' said Madge. 'I once went to a yoga and meditation retreat in India. It was magic.'

'I'm not sure meditating is my thing,' said Esther. 'I don't think I could sit for very long and do nothing.'

'But that's the point,' said Mabel excitedly. 'If you listened to what Flappy was saying, you're not doing nothing. You're travelling. Yes, you're a traveller, setting out on an adventure into your deepest self.'

'I'm not sure I have one of those,' said Esther.

'Everyone does,' said Madge. 'The secret to Enlightenment is to find it.'

'I'd like to write in here,' interjected Sally. 'Such a perfect place to create.'

'If you meditate you might find you're more inspired, Sally,' said Mabel. 'What do you say, Flappy? Can we join your meditation club?'

Flappy was not aware that she *had* a meditation club. She swayed a little, steadied herself on the Buddha, and then said, 'Once Gerald has redecorated and completed my shrine, we shall see.'

The following morning, Flappy awoke at fifteen minutes past nine with a headache. She put a hand to her forehead and groaned. She had not, for as far back as her memory stretched, which was very far, had a hangover. Hangovers were for people who could not control themselves. For people without restraint or dignity. Flappy was not one of those. At least she hadn't been, up until now. She stared at the clock on her bedside table, blinked a couple of times, and then stared at it again. It couldn't be past nine o'clock. It simply couldn't. She hadn't slept in like this since she was a teenager. Sleeping in was for people like Kenneth. People who snored and had big bellies and filled their days with nothing but golf. It was not for lithe, slender, yoga-practising people like Flappy.

Slowly, Flappy sat up and swung her legs over the side of the bed. Persephone would be in the hall and Kenneth would be getting up, she thought with a sinking feeling. She wondered how she could pretend she'd been up since five, but her usually sharp and busy mind felt sluggish and empty and no bright idea popped into it. She dragged her heavy feet along the carpet to the bathroom. She could tell by the smell of toothpaste that Kenneth was already up. Kenneth had never got up before her in all the years they'd been married. Flappy had made a point of it. No man should witness a woman with sleep in her eyes and morning breath. If there was one thing she was very good at, it was looking and smelling her best at the breakfast table.

Flappy was horrified by the sight that confronted her in the bathroom mirror. She gasped. The old woman in the glass gasped too, put a hand to her mouth and stared back in panic. Blinking a few times did not make her go away. Flappy dug deep, as only Flappy could, and found her determination. Never before had she needed it like she needed it now. With single-mindedness and unwavering focus, she set about repairing the damage done by an evening of heavy drinking. She washed her face, she brushed her teeth, then she went to her vanity table where the hard work would take place. Now was not the time to joke about the portrait in the attic, for the portrait was right here, staring out at her from the mirror.

At ten o'clock Flappy went downstairs. She'd put on a pair of casual trousers and a blue, open-neck shirt, adorning her ears, neck and wrists with her usual gold jewellery. Her hair was sleek and her skin, if not glowing with its typical radiance, was at least even. Besides mascara there was little she could do with her eyes, which were bloodshot, so she covered them up with a glamorous pair of big sunglasses. There was no point denying she'd had too much to drink, she might as well make a feature of it.

Persephone was in the library at her desk, being busy. When Flappy appeared, she stopped what she was doing and stood up. 'Good morning, Mrs Scott-Booth,' she said, knowing it would be impolite to ask her how she was.

'Good morning, Persephone,' said Flappy. 'I'm afraid I had a teeny bit too much to drink last night with the girls. I'm paying for it this morning.'

'You'd never know,' said Persephone tactfully.

Flappy gave a wan smile. 'You're very sweet, Persephone, but I'm afraid I'm going to have to wear sunglasses inside, which I never *ever* do. Only minor celebrities and vain and insecure film stars wear sunglasses inside. It's frightfully common, but I'm left no choice. My eyes look like a bloodhound's.'

'Would you like me to drive into town and buy you some eye drops? I know a brand that really works for hangover eyes.'

'Do you?' said Flappy, hope flaring in her heart. She did so hate looking like a bloodhound.

'Absolutely. I'll go right now, if you like.'

'That would be very kind, thank you.'

'Mrs Harvey-Smith called asking whether you'd be on for

bridge this evening. She said she's invited a couple of very good players and would love you to partner her, as you play better than everyone else.'

Flappy's spirits perked up. 'Did she say that? How sweet of her. Well, I did rather show them all a clean pair of heels last week. Call her back and tell her that I'd love to come once I've wriggled out of my late afternoon meeting.'

Persephone looked puzzled. She began searching the diary. 'Which meeting is that, Mrs Scott-Booth . . . ?'

'There is no meeting, Persephone. If working for me will teach you anything, which I hope it will, you will learn that it always pays to look busy, especially when you aren't. No one wants people who are not in demand. People who no one else wants.'

'Ah, I see,' said Persephone.

'I'm going to get something to eat. I'm feeling rather queasy this morning. I hope I feel better in time for bridge. I don't want to let Hedda down.' And she wandered off towards the kitchen.

Kenneth was at the kitchen table, reading *The Times*. The *Daily Mail* was on the island. 'Ah, morning, darling. Are you all right? I thought you might have died in the night, but then, as you were breathing, I realized you hadn't and that you'd probably had a big night. So I left you to sleep it off.'

Flappy frowned. 'What time did you come home? And, remind me where you went?'

'I went to the golfing dinner at the club, the one you didn't want to come to,' he replied.

Flappy put a hand to her head. 'Oh.' She couldn't remember anything about it.

Kenneth chuckled. 'You'd passed out by the time I came home.'

'Had I?'

'Yes, you were lying on the bed in your clothes.'

Flappy's jaw dropped. 'In my clothes?' She sat down.

'Yes, in your clothes. I put you into your pyjamas and tucked you up in bed.'

Flappy was appalled. How incredibly undignified. She put a hand to her chest as a flourish of heat spread across her face. 'You put me to bed?'

He gave her an amused look. 'Darling, I am your husband. Who else was going to put you to bed?'

She took a deep breath. 'I don't know what to say,' she said. If there was one thing she was usually very good at, it was knowing the right thing to say.

'There's nothing to say. You had a heavy night with the girls. I'm sure you had a lot of fun.' He put a hand on hers. 'To be honest, I'm glad you got drunk. You need to let your hair down sometimes.'

'Well, I let it all down last night, didn't I?'

'You did.' He then laughed, the kind of laugh that has been suppressed and suddenly bursts out. 'You called me Beastie,' he said.

Flappy blanched. 'Beastie?'

'Yes, Beastie.'

'Good Lord.' She was about to swoon.

'I don't ever recall you calling me Beastie,' said Kenneth,

who was very happy with the name. 'But you can call me Beastie again, if you like. I think it suits me.'

Flappy tried to smile. 'The things one says in one's sleep . . . ' she mumbled.

'And, by the way, the *Daily Mail* arrived with *The Times*. Must be some mistake. I asked Persephone if it was hers, but, as I thought, she's much too highbrow to read that kind of rag.'

'I'll let the delivery man know.'

'And take it easy today,' he said, getting up.

'I will.'

He grinned at her broadly. 'Beastie's going to play golf.'

Persephone drove into town to buy Flappy's eye drops. It was a lovely early autumn day. The wind was slightly crisp but the sun was shining brightly on the blackberry bushes as she drove down the winding lanes towards Badley Compton. She parked the car on the kerb outside Café Délice and got out. Just as she was about to set off down the road, Mabel Hitchens popped out. 'Persephone,' she said, glancing up and down the street, 'can I grab you for a moment?'

Persephone was perplexed. Mabel looked anxious. 'Of course. I'm just going to buy something at Boots for Mrs Scott-Booth.'

'That can wait. Come inside and have a coffee with me.' She almost took Persephone by the hand and led her into the café.

Esther, Madge and Sally were at a corner table. When they

saw Persephone they smiled and pulled up another chair. Persephone greeted them and sat down.

'What'll you have?' Mabel asked.

'A caffè latte would be nice, thank you,' she replied. Mabel went to the counter to ask Big Mary for a caffè latte and another round of coffees for herself, Esther, Madge and Sally.

'Beautiful day,' said Sally, as they waited for Mabel to return to the table.

'Beautiful,' Persephone agreed.

'I always think spring and autumn are the prettiest seasons,' said Madge.

'Me too,' Esther agreed. 'January and February are punishing, especially if you're out on a horse every day. Still, someone's got to do it.'

Mabel came back and sat down. 'So,' she said in an officious tone of voice. 'We need to talk to you about Flappy.'

'Oh,' said Persephone uncomfortably, feeling disloyal suddenly.

'Flappy is not herself at the moment,' said Esther. 'She's gone very weird and is doing weird, out-of-character things, like getting drunk.'

'Yes, she does look hungover this morning,' Persephone agreed.

'You're with her every day. We thought you might know what's going on,' said Sally.

Persephone shrugged. She did not want to be indiscreet, but then, these women were Flappy's best friends. Perhaps they were right in being concerned about her. It was true, Flappy had been acting weirdly.

'I've only just started working for Mrs Scott-Booth,' said Persephone. 'So, I'm not sure what is normal. But I can tell you that she has taken to meditating every evening at five.'

'On her own?' asked Mabel.

'Well, I'm looking for a guru to teach her how to do it properly, but so far I haven't found one. Gurus don't grow on trees in Badley Compton.'

'You need an Indian,' said Madge firmly. 'Flappy will want to be authentic.'

'How long does she meditate for?' asked Sally.

'I'm not sure. I knock off at six and she's not back. An hour and a half? Two hours?'

The four women looked at each other thoughtfully while Big Mary put their drinks on the table.

'Is everything okay between her and Kenneth?' asked Madge, when Big Mary was gone.

'I think so,' Persephone replied. 'Mr Scott-Booth plays golf every morning but comes back for lunch. They have breakfast and lunch together every day. They seem happy.'

'So, she's not having an affair?' chuckled Esther.

'Esther!' cried Mabel. 'You can't say that! If there's one person in Badley Compton who won't be having an affair, it's Flappy.' She turned to Persephone. 'Flappy is a woman of high principles and moral standards,' she told her loftily.

'She's distracted,' said Sally.

'And vague,' said Madge.

'And unusually happy,' added Esther.

'Isn't she normally happy?' asked Persephone.

'Not *this* happy. This is more than happy,' said Esther.

'This is a state of bliss,' said Madge, nodding slowly to show that she knew what a state of bliss looked like because of her retreat in India. 'If it's meditation, then she's going somewhere ordinary people don't go.'

Mabel sighed. 'I normally speak to her on the telephone every day, but she hasn't been calling me.'

'She's becoming quite friendly with Mrs Harvey-Smith,' said Persephone.

'Flappy is not the sort of person to drop her friends because someone more important turns up. Flappy's not like that,' said Mabel, wondering secretly whether dropping her friends was just another example of the peculiar change in Flappy.

Persephone left them finishing their coffee and walked out into the sunshine. She headed off to the chemist for the eye drops, musing on Flappy's friends and how little they really knew her. What Flappy said and what she did were two very different things, but these women were impressed, as Flappy wanted them to be. Persephone had a pretty good idea what had come over Flappy, but she wasn't about to share that idea with anyone. It was enough to stand on the sidelines and watch how it developed. Meditation? Did they *really* think it was that?

'Meditation,' said Mabel decisively. 'That's what it is. But how is she doing it, all alone, without a guru?'

'We need to find out,' said Madge.

'Let's spy on her,' suggested Sally, shivering with excitement.

The three women stared at her in horror. But then, as they processed it, their horror lifted and was replaced by a sense of intrigue and mischief. They looked at each other guiltily. 'What if she discovers us?' asked Madge nervously, dropping her voice to a whisper.

'She won't,' said Sally firmly. 'We'll be careful. We'll park at the edge of the property, behind the cottage, and creep through the wood. We can peep in through the window. If she's meditating she'll have her eyes closed.'

'Good point,' said Esther.

'All right,' Madge agreed.

'And if she *were* to discover us, we could say we're spying out of concern,' said Mabel.

'Exactly,' agreed Sally.

'We just want the old Flappy back,' said Mabel, and they nodded their agreement. They *all* wanted that.

Chapter 11

Flappy did not feel well. She went into the garden and lay on one of the sun loungers. When Persephone returned from Badley Compton with the eye drops, she found her boss asleep with the *Spectator* lying across her chest. Concerned that Flappy was going to get sunburnt, Persephone moved the parasol so that her face was no longer in the sun. Even though it was early September the sun was still hot and quite ferocious and she knew how much Flappy cherished her skin. It was on account of that small gesture that when Flappy stirred from her slumber her face was not lobster red, but lightly flushed. The snooze had done her good and she was feeling better.

'I bumped into your friends in Big Mary's,' Persephone told her when Flappy came inside.

'Which ones? I have so many friends in Badley Compton.'

'Mrs Hitchens, Mrs Hancock, Mrs Tennant and Mrs Armitage,' Persephone replied.

'Ah, a veritable coven. I suppose they were talking about me,' said Flappy, fanning herself with the magazine. 'It's still hot out there, isn't it? What a summer we've had.'

'They asked how you were,' Persephone replied carefully.

'As well they might. I suppose I did get a teeny bit tiddly last night. Very unlike me. I never *ever* get tiddly.' She smiled and there was a touch of delight in it. 'I think it's imperative to let one's hair down occasionally, don't you, Persephone? Life's very dull if one is always on one's best behaviour, and who better to let one's hair down with than one's closest friends?'

'You're right,' said Persephone. She had only worked for Mrs Scott-Booth for a couple of weeks but knew already that the best policy was always to agree. She had learned that from Kenneth, who was a master.

'Tonight I'm playing bridge with Mrs Harvey-Smith,' Flappy reminded her. 'I'll be doing my usual meditation at five. Remember, no one must disturb me. That's very important. If one is going to go deep into one's subconscious, one must not be jolted out of it by a clumsy intruder.'

'Don't worry, Mrs Scott-Booth. Everyone here knows not to disturb you.'

'Yes,' said Flappy. 'We are so *so* lucky. The staff are very considerate here at Darnley.'

Flappy felt better, but still not a hundred per cent. More like seventy, if she really thought about it, which she did because she didn't have anything else to do today. Had she done her yoga, she would feel balanced and serene, she knew. Had she swum and danced naked she would have felt that wonderful sense of euphoria again that had propelled her through the last week. But no, she had got drunk and, because of her lack of self-control, was now feeling leaden inside. Nothing seemed able to lighten it. Not even the thought of Charles, doing all those deliciously naughty things to her, managed to lift her spirits. She decided she would spend the afternoon in her bedroom, wander down to the cottage for a meditation with her Buddha at five and then drive to Hedda's for bridge at seven. She was loath to cancel Charles, but it couldn't be helped. Beauty was not her best today and Beastie deserved only the best.

While Flappy slept in her darkened room, Persephone was busy in the library working on the jumble sale, the Harvest Festival tea, the Halloween children's fancy dress parade, Bonfire Night, plus replying to all the emails Flappy received with regard to the parish committee and various other committees and groups that Flappy was part of. She answered the telephone, liaised with the gardeners, and Karen and Tatiana, and generally took over the running of Darnley, which took some running being such a big and beautiful place. And all the while Flappy slept, and dreamed of Charles and how she was going to shine at the bridge table tonight, because she was, it must be acknowledged, an exceedingly good player.

When Flappy awoke she was almost back to her normal ebullient self. Her liver had repaired itself as healthy livers like hers tend to do and her eyes were no longer bloodshot. She did not need dark glasses to hide the bloodhound. The bloodhound was gone. She just needed a teeny bit of make-up, a herbal tea, perhaps a banana and honey and then she'd feel well again.

And so it was with a bounce in her step and the scent of roses in her nostrils that she made her way through the many manicured gardens to the cottage for her meditation. She rather regretted cancelling Charles, because now she felt up for it. Still, perhaps an hour of contemplation would push her up to one hundred per cent, so that she'd really be on form for Hedda's bridge game. After all, there were plenty of evenings to be had with Charles. They stretched out into the horizon, and over it, in a series of heavenly rendezvous of which there seemed no end. Was it possible to wear out one's body with so much activity, she wondered as she put the key in the lock and turned it.

Flappy lit the tea lights and the four incense sticks that Gerald had carefully placed around the Buddha in pretty ceramic holders. She attached her Apple phone to the speaker and turned on the New Age music Persephone had selected for her, which was played against the sound of a stream trickling through a forest. Delightfully soothing, she thought. Lastly, she sprinkled the flowers she had picked on the way at the Buddha's feet – she considered that quite authentic – slipped out of her shoes and sat cross-legged on the bright orange cushion that Gerald had bought especially. Really, Gerald was so attentive, she reflected as she settled into the lotus position. She wondered when he was going to arrange for the walls to be painted and which fabrics he was going to suggest for the curtains and blinds. Perhaps she should change the carpet too. She imagined Gerald had thought of that. Gerald thought of everything. Then, as she put her hands on her knees and lightly joined her thumbs with her forefingers, she thought how lucky she was to be able to sit in this position, because most of the women she knew, and men, of course, were too stiff to even attempt it. But years of yoga had kept Flappy supple. Very supple. So supple, in fact, that she could hold this position for hours if she needed to. Flappy never *ever* boasted, but it would be erroneous not to acknowledge that she had the body of a much younger woman.

While Flappy closed her eyes and tried to still her busy mind, which was quite impossible considering how very busy it was, Mabel, Madge, Esther and Sally arrived in Mabel's car and parked on the edge of the property a short distance behind the cottage. Quietly and nervously they climbed out. 'Do you think we're doing the right thing?' asked Madge, suddenly wishing she were anywhere but here.

Mabel turned on her. In the absence of Flappy taking control, Mabel was turning out to be a bit of a tyrant. 'Do you want the old Flappy back?' she demanded.

'Yes,' said Madge with certainty. She did not much like the new Mabel, either.

'Then come along.' Mabel looked at her watch. 'It's quarter past five. She must be at it by now.'

The other two did not protest and followed Mabel up the path that snaked its way through the trees. The afternoon light was turning a rich shade of gold and they trod softly over the dappled ground, trying not to make a sound. 'Shhh!' hissed Mabel as Esther stood loudly on a branch. Mabel put her finger across her lips. Esther pulled a 'sorry' face, but as soon as Mabel's back was turned she rolled her eyes to Sally and Madge. Sally and Madge smiled in sympathy.

At last they arrived at the back of the cottage. In spite of Mabel being in charge, her heart began to thump. She put a hand on her chest, hoping to stifle the sound. They stood, the four of them, pressed up against the wall. Madge felt sick. She did not want to be caught by Flappy. Sally was as nervous as the others, but the small risk of getting caught would be worth it as she could put the adventure into one of her books. Esther was ready to blame the entire escapade on Mabel, were Flappy to discover them. They waited for Mabel to give the order. Mabel hesitated, wondering in a sudden flash of clarity whether this really was such a good idea. Then Esther lifted her hand. They had come this far, after all, she thought. They might as well follow the plan through to the end. 'Come on,' she said, and without waiting for the other three began to edge her way round the corner.

Flappy's mind was like a rebellious cricket. The more she told it to still, the more it hopped about, as if it did so just to spite her. She tried focusing on the music, then she focused on her breathing, finally she tried to imagine every thought as a cloud wafting across her mind. But the clouds turned into sheep and they began frolicking about in an annoying, out-of-control sort of way, and she was unable to conjure up a sheepdog to herd them all into line again. There was only one thing for it. She would have to try 'Om'.

As Esther's face peeped in through the bottom left-hand corner of the window, Flappy began to chant 'Om'. There was something about the vibration in her chest that was really quite pleasing. *Yes*, she thought excitedly, *this feels very nice indeed*. She took another breath. 'Oooouuuummmmm,' she went in a long, buzzing hum that began behind her ribs and came out through her nose. 'Oooouuuummmmm.'

Mabel, Madge and Sally joined Esther at the window. With wide, incredulous eyes, they watched Flappy in amazement. There she was, sitting in the Lotus position in a fog of incense and candlelight, chanting happily to herself. The ecstatic expression on her face confirmed what Madge had known all along, that Flappy had reached Nirvana. She had stilled her busy mind and descended into the very core of her being, the secret chamber of her subconscious, the very essence of her soul; Flappy had united with the Source.

The women were unable to tear themselves away. It was a thrilling sight, after all, to see someone reach Enlightenment, and they were transfixed. Each woman silently questioned whether this blissful state was something *she* could achieve, or whether it was only possible for high-minded, superior people like Flappy. After what seemed like a very long time, Mabel tugged Esther's sleeve. She gave her a look. Esther nodded and nudged Sally, who prodded Madge. They edged away from the window and back to the car the way they had come. Midges hovered in the fading light, the air grew damp and an autumn chill blew in off the sea. It was a while before they spoke. The sight had rendered them speechless, and a little disappointed; it did not look like they were ever going to get the old Flappy back.

At five minutes to seven Flappy turned into Compton Court in her Range Rover, singing along to Dolly Parton's '9 To

5'. She parked outside the front door, smoothed down her hair in the mirror, pinched her cheeks and smiled, for her meditation had given her a youthful glow and she was feeling quite pleased with herself. Johnson greeted her at the door. They exchanged pleasantries and Johnson gave her a smile that, while retaining the appropriate distance between butler and guest, made her feel like she belonged there at Compton, as a dear friend of his mistress. Flappy was shown into the drawing room, for the evenings were too chilly now for sitting on the terrace. Hedda, who'd been perching on the club fender, got up to greet her. 'Flappy!' she exclaimed, smiling happily. 'How lovely to see you.'

'It's lovely to be here,' Flappy replied graciously. The two women held hands and kissed each other on the cheek.

'I do love your scent, Flappy,' said Hedda. 'Every time you go anywhere, you leave a cloud of tuberose behind you.'

'It's Jo Malone,' said Flappy grandly.

'Of course it is,' said Hedda. 'Jo Malone's tuberose is unmistakable.' She turned to the other two ladies seated on the sofas. 'You know Mary, of course, but I don't think you know Amanda Worthington?' Flappy was surprised that she didn't. She knew pretty much everyone in Badley Compton. 'Amanda lives in Appledore,' Hedda continued. *Well, that explains it,* thought Flappy. She did not know everyone in Appledore.

Flappy shook Amanda's thin hand and took in her blowsy hair and bland, lifeless face and thought she looked like a dried-flower arrangement that has spent too many years on a windowsill in the sun so that all the colours have faded to a lacklustre beige. However, when Amanda spoke, Flappy realized that she was very posh. Not aristocratic, like Hedda and Lady Micklethwaite, but a notch below. Upper middle class, to be exact, and Flappy did like to be exact in these matters. Amanda wore no discernible make-up and displayed discreet, delicate jewellery on her small wrists and ears, jewellery passed down through the family that really should have been banished to the back of a drawer for its lack of flair. If there was one thing Flappy was good at, it was dressing with flair. Amanda Worthington had none.

Flappy sat in one of the armchairs and when Johnson asked her quietly what she would like to drink, she replied just loud enough for Amanda to hear, 'Something soft, Johnson, thank you. You know me so well, I trust you to make me something nice.'

Johnson did not know Flappy at all well, but he did not blink. Instead, he nodded and replied smoothly, 'Of course, Mrs Scott-Booth. Leave it to me.' A few minutes later he returned with an elderflower cordial garnished with mint, on a silver tray.

'Lovely,' Flappy gushed, taking the crystal glass and smiling up at him warmly. 'Thank you, Johnson.'

Flappy made polite conversation with Amanda, but it was a challenge. The woman was nice enough, but goodness she was dull. Flappy wished she were sitting on the other armchair, closest to Hedda and Big Mary. The two of *them* were laughing heartily with the intimacy of family members, even though they had only discovered each other some five months before. Flappy couldn't help admiring Hedda for including Big Mary, who, it had to be acknowledged, was very common. With her platinum hair and leggings, not to mention her Devon brogue, she should have been out of place here at Compton Court, with the niece of a marquess. However, Hedda had no airs. Sure, she was strident, confident, and entitled in that 'to the manor born' way, but she was not a snob. If Flappy hated one thing above all others, it was a snob. Proper posh people were not snobs, only those not quite there looked down their noses at the lesser folk. Flappy would never *ever* do that. After all, the Duchess of Devonshire was gracious to everyone and Flappy admired her very much, and believed that, although she did not like to boast, she and the Duchess were really quite similar.

It was a relief when Hedda announced that it was time for bridge. 'I might just nip to the loo,' said Flappy, who did not need it but had heard Charles's voice in the distance, talking to Johnson. 'Won't be a minute,' she said, hurrying out. She followed the sound of Charles's clipped vowels, across the hall and down a corridor and on into unfamiliar territory. Sure enough, there he was, holding a painting in a gilt frame.

'Flappy,' he exclaimed and his beautiful green eyes lit up.

'Surely not a surprise,' she said, smiling flirtatiously.

'No, I knew you were coming. I'm glad you sneaked out.'

'I wanted to say hello.'

'I missed you today,' he said, lowering his voice.

'I missed you too.'

He put the painting on the floor and leant it against the wall, leaving his hands free to take Flappy by the

153

waist. He kissed her on the mouth. 'You smell delicious, Beauty,' he said.

'So do you, Beastie.' But as she said it Kenneth's red face materialized in front of her eyes. She blinked him away.

'I want you,' said Charles, and the urgency in his voice made something in Flappy's stomach flutter.

'We must wait until tomorrow,' she said.

'I can't.'

'You must.' Flappy panicked suddenly that he was going to take her right there in the corridor.

He grinned and Flappy went weak. 'I will find a way. Leave it to me.'

'I'd better get back to the drawing room before they miss me,' said Flappy, wriggling out of his grasp.

'I'll see you later.' Flappy gave him a stern look, which only made him more ardent. 'I will,' he said firmly, his face full of mischief. 'It's *my* house and I'll do what I want. You'll see.'

Flappy returned to the drawing room to find the women already seated at the table. 'Come on, Flappy,' said Hedda. 'You're my partner, so you'd better be on form.'

'Oh, I *am* on form,' said Flappy, who was now fired up and about to burst with excitement. How was Charles going to engineer a tryst tonight? she wondered. And in his house too, with Hedda, Big Mary and Amanda sitting in here, oblivious. How incredibly exciting! She turned her mind to the cards. She did not want to let Hedda down and she certainly did not want to be outshone by the boring old dried-flower arrangement. However, as they began to play it transpired that Amanda was a demon at bridge. The dried-flower arrangement came to life and suddenly the beige was transformed to a competitive scarlet and the woman who had nothing interesting to say grew lively and, Flappy had to concede, witty too, as she wiped the table with them all.

At the end of the game, Flappy had to pretend that she didn't mind losing; after all, only lesser mortals lost their tempers when they didn't win. Flappy most certainly was not one of them. She was gracious and charming, although, it must be said, she had to dig deep to find those qualities in herself. Mrs Ellis had made a delicious light supper and the four women sat around the kitchen table, discussing the game in a lively post-mortem.

It was at the end of supper, when Flappy was sipping a fresh mint tea and Hedda was enjoying a bottle of sweet dessert wine, shared by Big Mary and Amanda, that Charles walked in. 'Good evening, girls,' he said in a cheerful voice, a turquoise cashmere sweater draped casually around his shoulders. He bent down and kissed them in turn. Flappy had to make a big effort not to give herself away. But when it came to acting, Flappy put Meryl Streep in the shade. She was truly gifted. She smiled in that charming, nonchalant way of hers and no one would have guessed at the things she and Charles got up to in the cottage.

After a brief chat, during which Hedda told him that she and Flappy had lost to Amanda and Big Mary, because she was yet to find a player who could out-play Amanda, Charles held up the painting. 'Darling, I'm trying to find a place to hang this,' he said. 'Perhaps you and your three friends can give me some advice.'

Hedda shook her head and chortled. 'Don't be silly. I haven't a clue.' She looked at Flappy. 'Ask Flappy. She's the only one around this table with an eye for that sort of thing. Would you mind, Flappy? You'd be doing me such a favour.'

Flappy looked bashful, which was quite an achievement for a woman who had never felt bashful in her life. 'I'm not sure I'm really qualified,' she said.

'You're much more qualified than any of us,' said Hedda.

'Come on, Flappy,' said Charles. 'You can be Badley Compton's Minister for Good Taste.'

Flappy put down her teacup. She already *was* Badley Compton's unofficial Minister for Good Taste, she thought wryly. 'Very well. If you really can't do it yourself,' she said, getting up.

'You're a darling,' said Hedda, refilling the three wine glasses. 'Thank you, Flappy.'

Flappy followed Charles out of the kitchen, astonished that he had come up with such an ingenious way to get her on her own. 'You're a devil,' she said in delight.

'A devil *and* a beast,' he laughed. 'I'm clearly a very dangerous man!'

He swiftly ascended the sweeping staircase, and Flappy had to admit that the staircase at Compton was grander than the one at Darnley, although Darnley, she felt (with satisfaction), had more charm. Flappy quickened her pace to keep up. 'There's a corridor up here where it might go nicely,' he said, turning to give her a wink.

'Oh, Beastie,' she gushed. 'You're so naughty!'

A moment later they were in a spare bedroom, the painting discarded on the carpet, making love on the big and bouncy four-poster bed. Flappy thought it was the most thrilling thing she had ever done. It was wicked beyond her most wicked dreams. To think that Charles Harvey-Smith was inside her while his wife, her niece and friend were downstairs in the kitchen in blissful ignorance. The excitement brought the episode to a quicker climax than normal, but Flappy was quite relieved. She did not want Hedda to discover them in flagrante delicto. Charles rolled off her and sighed with pleasure. 'I'm a beast!' he exclaimed.

Flappy stared up at the ceiling of the four-poster bed, which was decorated with panels of pretty paintings, faded with the passing of centuries, and wondered why they didn't have a bed like this at Darnley. 'I can't believe you pulled it off,' she said.

'I told you I would.'

'Yes, you did.'

'It's *my* house and you're *my* mistress. I'll take you whenever I want.'

Flappy felt a frisson of excitement. She had never been anyone's mistress before. Besides, the word 'mistress' implied a young and sexy woman with curves in all the right places. She was flattered. 'In your own home, too. I'd never have thought you'd have the nerve.'

'If I were a younger man, I'd do it again.'

'What? Now?'

'Yes, Beauty, now. If we were in our twenties, I wouldn't put you down.'

She caught her breath. 'Beastie, you're unstoppable!'

Charles looked down to find, to his surprise, that his excitement was rising again. 'Good Lord!' he exclaimed. 'Are you ready for another round, Beauty?'

Chapter 12

As the evening of Hedda and Charles's party approached, Flappy turned her busy mind to a trivial but highly important matter. What was she going to wear? It was a question fraught with possibility. On the one hand Flappy had a reputation to uphold for she was without doubt the best-dressed woman in Badley Compton. That was an undisputed fact, like Big Mary made the best cakes and Mabel Hitchens was the best gossip. However, on the other hand, Flappy, being a sensitive and tactful soul, did not want to make other people, especially her hostess who was fast becoming one of her most intimate friends, uncomfortable. In short, Flappy did not want to outshine to the point of blinding. She wanted to look elegant, tasteful, with a touch of her inimitable (although Mabel tried very hard) flair, but at the same time she wanted to look approachable. That was not going to be easy.

'Persephone,' she called from the hall five days before the party. Persephone duly appeared, with an alert, ready-for-anything expression on her face. Flappy was getting quite accustomed to the girl's face and decided that she liked it very much. It was intelligent, and, being an intelligent person herself, Flappy appreciated a quick and agile mind. 'I need to buy a dress for Hedda's party. I have nothing suitable in my wardrobe. I'd like you to come with me and help me find something in town.' Town did not mean Badley Compton. There certainly wasn't anything suitable to be found *there*. Town was Chestminster, which was a forty-minute drive north.

Flappy and Persephone set off in Flappy's car. Flappy played classical music. 'I have a loathing for pop music,' she said, which Persephone knew wasn't true because a few days before Flappy had asked her to fill her car up with petrol and, as soon as she'd started the engine, Celine Dion's 'Think Twice' had blared out of the CD player. However, Persephone knew how best to answer her boss.

'I agree with you, Mrs Scott-Booth,' she said. 'Classical music is so refined. I'm afraid most people, especially people my age, don't have the fine, cultured mind that you have and would rather sing along to Radio One.'

'The ill-educated masses,' said Flappy with a sigh. 'They'll get there,' she added generously. 'We are all on our spiritual path, aren't we? It doesn't matter how long we take or by which road we travel, we will all get there in the end.' She gave a little sniff because *she* was in Fast Track and would get there a darnn sight quicker than everyone else.

'You're so right,' Persephone agreed. 'How are you finding your meditation?'

'Just wonderful,' enthused Flappy. 'Sometimes I go so far away, I fear I might not come back.'

'That wouldn't be good.'

'No, I'd be dead,' said Flappy with a laugh, because since taking up with Charles she found everything funny.

Persephone laughed too. 'I'm sure that's a very rare occurrence.'

'Still, I do need to keep a grip on reality, Persephone,' she said seriously. 'What's that saying: one mustn't be too heavenly minded so as to be no earthly good?'

'Quite,' Persephone agreed. 'By the way, I'm still trying to find you a guru. It's not easy in Badley Compton. There are a few possibilities, but I need to find out whether they're the real deal or simply charlatans out to take advantage of you.'

'Goodness, that would be dreadful. One is so vulnerable when one is far away.'

They arrived in Chestminster, a cathedral town which boasted, besides a magnificent Gothic cathedral, a John Lewis and a Starbucks coffee shop. Flappy parked in the municipal car park and then marched down the pedestrianized street to the shop that never failed her, Chic Boutique. The owner, a small, tidy woman in late middle age, just happened to be in today, and, when she saw Flappy, embraced her like a long-lost friend. 'Mrs Scott-Booth, what a lovely surprise,' she gushed, and then greeted Persephone politely. By the attention she lavished on Flappy, it was clear that she did not expect Persephone to be spending any money.

'I've brought my PA with me, Cheryl,' said Flappy grandly. 'Persephone has a jolly good eye for this sort of thing and I value her opinion. I need a dress for a party.'

'What kind of party?' asked Cheryl.

'It's a cocktail party at Compton Court. The last party of the summer,' said Flappy.

'So you need something between seasons. The evenings are drawing in now and it's getting quite chilly when the sun's down. Come, let me show you what we have.'

Flappy followed Cheryl to a rail of dresses while Persephone answered her mobile phone. It was Gerald, arranging a time that afternoon to bring round his designs for the cottage. 'Three would be perfect,' said Persephone.

'Make it four,' interrupted Flappy, who had cocked an ear to their conversation. If Gerald was at the cottage when Charles arrived it would give their meeting an air of respectability. To hide in plain sight, she thought to herself with satisfaction. She would send Charles a text to warn him.

Flappy pulled out four possibilities and Cheryl hung them up in the changing room. 'Can I bring you a cup of coffee?' she asked.

'Lovely,' said Flappy. 'And one for Persephone. I keep her so busy she needs sustenance, don't you, Persephone?'

'Absolutely,' she replied. 'Thank you very much.'

Persephone sat on the pink upholstered sofa and sipped her coffee while Flappy came out in each creation. Persephone had to hand it to her. Everything she put on looked wonderful on her. She just had that kind of willowy body that suited clothes.

'Oh, that blue is your colour,' gushed Cheryl when Flappy flounced out in a deep indigo dress that accentuated her slim waist and hips beautifully.

Flappy admired herself in the mirror. 'Yes, it does seem

to be my colour, doesn't it,' she agreed, liking her reflection very much.

'Everything looks good on you, Mrs Scott-Booth,' Persephone said truthfully. 'Did you ever model?'

Flappy screwed up her nose in distaste. 'No,' she replied. 'You see, I've always been fortunate to have a good brain. Modelling is for shallow women who have nothing to offer but their beauty. I would never *ever* rely solely on that. Beauty fades, after all.' She put a hand to her face. 'I'm so *so* lucky that mine hasn't faded yet.' Then she added in her usual self-deprecating manner, because Flappy was loath to boast, 'Of course, it will eventually. Time catches up with us all in the end, doesn't it.'

Flappy was delighted with the blue dress. It was perfect. Elegant for the women and subtly sexy for Charles. With her gold jewellery and a shawl she had at home that would complement it beautifully, it would cement her position as the best-dressed woman in Badley Compton. Just as she was about to leave the shop, her telephone pinged with a text. She took it out of her handbag, put on her reading glasses, and had a look. It was from Charles. 'Good morning, B. I'm a devil today. Looking forward to 5 p.m. I hope you're ready for me.'

Flappy felt a stirring in her loins. She was ready for him now. 'Darling B, I'm always ready for *you*. Counting down the hours till five.'

She turned to Persephone. 'Let's buy *you* a dress too,' she said, for she was now in an exceedingly good mood and generous with it.

163

'Really?' said Persephone in surprise.

'Cheryl, what do you have for Persephone?'

Half an hour and two further cups of coffee later, Persephone left the shop with her boss carrying two large shopping bags and wearing a big smile. 'You're so kind, Mrs Scott-Booth,' she said for the tenth time.

'You deserve it,' said Flappy. 'You work very hard and I always reward where a reward is due.'

'Well, thank you. It's just so generous of you to think of me.'

'It's my pleasure, after all, my daughters are grown-up now and living on the other side of the world. Even when they lived at home they were hard to buy for.' An unpleasant memory surfaced then of a fight the three of them had had in London, on the second floor of Harvey Nichols, because everything Flappy had pulled off the rail they had hated and everything *they* had pulled off the rail Flappy had refused to pay for. Persephone had accepted the dress Flappy chose for her and had said a very heartfelt thank you afterwards. Now, that was the kind of shopping Flappy enjoyed. It was a shame her daughters hadn't been more like Persephone.

They stopped at a coffee shop on the way to the car park and Flappy bought them both a cake. 'Tell me,' she said as they took the table for two by the window. 'When did you last have a boyfriend?'

'I split up with Zac a year ago. We'd been going out for four years. We met at uni.'

'Oh, that's a long time. Did he break your heart?'

'It had run its course. We both knew that. But still, it was hard on both of us. I miss him, but I don't regret that we broke up.'

'One day, when you're happy with someone else, you'll look back and thank your stars that you aren't with Zac.'

Persephone pulled a sad face. 'I hope so, Mrs Scott-Booth. The trouble is, there aren't any men I fancy in Badley Compton.'

'It's a small pond, I agree,' said Flappy thoughtfully. 'You need to spread your net a little wider.'

Persephone shrugged. 'How?'

'Leave it to me. I'll find you someone.'

'Really?' Persephone laughed. Flappy had already generously bought her a dress and a cake, it seemed too much to expect her to find her a boyfriend too.

Flappy was insistent. 'If anyone can find you a boyfriend, Persephone,' she said, 'it's me.'

'How?'

'Contacts,' Flappy added mysteriously. 'It's all about who one knows and I know everyone.'

Flappy arrived home in time for lunch. Karen had made a delicious Vietnamese dish of fish, vegetables and steamed rice. It was so good that Flappy decided she'd invite the girls round for a Vietnamese-themed dinner and pretend that she'd cooked it. They'd be very impressed with Vietnamese fish.

Kenneth had enjoyed a good morning on the golf course. When he told her who he'd been playing with and the list did not include Charles, Flappy lost interest. Kenneth was a little surprised. He'd got used to her questioning him about his game, his form and his conversations. However, she told him that she'd bought a new dress in town and that explained it. She was distracted today, which was understandable. Hedda and Charles's party was but five days away and Kenneth knew just how much thought went into Flappy's wardrobe.

After lunch, Flappy was in her bedroom, laying out her new dress on the bed with the co-ordinating shawl, when the telephone rang. She was so distracted by the fantasy she was having of arriving at Compton Court for the party and turning every head on the lawn that she forgot to leave it ringing the habitual eight times. When she picked it up after the second ring, Mabel's voice came down the line in a torrent of enthusiasm. 'Flappy, I've news!' she exclaimed. As Mabel hadn't heard from Flappy for a few days, this piece of news was designed to pique her interest and remind her of Mabel's usefulness, for useful Mabel was when it came to the town gossip and keeping Flappy informed. Big Mary had told her about her bridge game at Hedda's house, which had included Flappy, and Mabel had been put out. Perhaps Flappy was, Mabel feared, dropping her old friends for her new one.

'I'm all ears. What's up?' said Flappy, sitting on the edge of the bed in preparation for this earth-shattering piece of information. For Mabel's voice implied nothing less.

'Guess who's coming to Hedda's party?'

Mabel's voice was trembling with excitement. Flappy's curiosity was indeed piqued, just as Mabel had hoped. 'I don't know. Who?'

'Monty Don!'

Flappy gasped. The celebrity gardener was indeed an excitement. Flappy had all of his books (although she'd only looked at the photographs) and had watched him on television. She had to admit, although not publicly because she was allergic to being like everyone else, that she *did* find him attractive. She was slightly put out, however, that Hedda had not told her herself. 'Well, that *is* news,' Flappy replied and Mabel's heart flooded with joy that she'd been able to tell her friend something she didn't already know.

'John got it from Big Mary this morning. Big Mary is a huge fan of Monty Don.' Mabel chuckled. 'Aren't we all!'

'He's a very impassioned horticulturalist,' said Flappy knowledgeably. She was damned if she was going to sink to the level of every other middle-aged woman in Badley Compton and comment on his looks. Commenting on people's looks was something Flappy never *ever* did. 'He has a brilliant mind,' she added loftily, to make the point. 'His books are incredibly informative. Have you read them, Mabel?' she asked.

'No, I haven't. I've just seen him on television. He's so handsome.'

'Is he?' said Flappy, sounding unconvinced.

'Oh, Flappy, you're much too high-minded,' said Mabel with a laugh. 'You didn't even notice how handsome Charles Harvey-Smith is.'

'He's an art collector, you know. What he doesn't know about art is nobody's business.'

'By the by, how's your meditation room coming along?' asked Mabel, changing the subject and blushing as she

167

mentioned it, for the embarrassment of having actually spied on her friend still stung.

'Gerald and I have been working on the designs. He's coming over this afternoon to discuss it with me. It's going to be divine.'

'Oh, you're so disciplined to be able to sit and meditate the way you do.'

'I've always been disciplined. After all, if one wasn't disciplined one would never get through all the things one has to do every day, being so terribly busy.'

'I really admire that about you, Flappy,' said Mabel, her guilt at having spied making her gush more than normal. 'By the by, what are you going to wear for the party?'

It irritated Flappy that Hedda's party was 'the party' and not 'Hedda's party'. 'Which party is that, Mabel?' she asked.

'Hedda's party.'

'Ah, yes, that party. No, I haven't given it a thought. I'm sure I can find something in my wardrobe.'

'If you don't, might you be nipping into Chic Boutique? They always have lovely things there,' said Mabel.

'Perhaps, if I have time. But really, one is so terribly busy.'

'Well, I won't keep you, Flappy,' she said, looking at her watch and ascertaining whether or not she had time to drive into Chestminster. 'Toodle-oo.'

At four o'clock Gerald arrived in his old Volvo Estate. The boot was full of rolls of fabric and wallpaper and boxes of samples and swatches. He appeared at Flappy's door with a black portfolio under his arm. Flappy greeted him warmly and took him straight to the cottage, stopping only briefly to admire a fat bumble bee toddling about the petals of a rose. On reflection, the roses really were very special at Darnley.

Once in the cottage, Gerald laid his portfolio on the table and unzipped it. He pulled out four mood boards. One for the downstairs, one for each of the two bedrooms, and the fourth for the bathrooms and sitting-room-kitchen. He'd taken the liberty of planning a total redecoration, knowing that Flappy would be easily persuaded to spend more of Kenneth's money than she'd previously expected. No one loved a decorating project more than Flappy.

Flappy looked at every board in turn while Gerald told her the idea behind each display of fabric and wall colours. They really were gorgeous, for Gerald had such a good eye.

'How are you finding the Buddha?' asked Gerald.

'Such an inspiration, Gerald,' Flappy replied. 'In fact, I must light the incense and candles before Charles gets here. You know he's my meditating partner?'

Gerald arched an eyebrow. 'What? Handsome Charles? Hedda's husband?'

'Is he handsome?' Flappy asked, giving him the wide-eyed, innocent look of someone who had never thought of it.

'Very,' said Gerald.

'Well, aren't I lucky then to have such a handsome meditation partner?' It suddenly occurred to Flappy that she had not remembered to send Charles a warning text. 'He'll be here in a minute.' She looked at her watch. Indeed, he'd be here in five.

'Oooh, goodie,' he cooed, hurrying to the Buddha to light the incense and candles. 'What does he think of your gorgeous statue?'

'Very conducive to meditation. He makes all the difference,' said Flappy, eyeing the door and hoping that Charles would make a discreet entrance.

Just as Gerald was bending down with the match the door flew open and Charles strode in like a gladiator who's just triumphed over lions at the Colosseum. 'Beastie here!' he exclaimed in a booming voice, a rose between his teeth. 'Where's Beauty?'

Flappy blanched. Gerald stood up, a startled expression on his face. Charles stared at Gerald as if he were a lion that had risen from the dead and slowly took the rose out of his mouth. There was a moment of excruciating awkwardness and then Flappy laughed. A light, nonchalant laugh. The laugh of a woman who knows her life depends on making light of this potentially damaging situation. If there was one thing Flappy was good at, it was turning something explosive into something benign. 'Oh, Charles, not Shakespeare again!' she said. Then she turned to Gerald. 'I told him you were going to be here, so *ce petit drame* must be for your benefit.' She didn't quite know why she'd broken into French. It must have been because she was deeply nervous.

Charles understood immediately and burst out laughing too. 'Gotcha!' he said, pointing at Gerald.

Gerald, whose face was a contortion of confusion, laughed too, although uneasily. 'Yes, you did,' he said, looking from Charles to Flappy and back again.

'Did you know that Charles used to be an actor?' she said.

'Shakespeare was one of my fortes,' said Charles, giving Gerald the benefit of his beautiful eyes and dazzling smile. 'That's an entrance from *Much Ado About Nothing.*' Which it wasn't, but Gerald had only read *Twelfth Night* at school and couldn't remember anything about it.

'Well, I would say don't give up your day job, but as you don't have one, I can't,' said Gerald, feeling a little tongue-tied suddenly in the face of such beauty. 'What do you think of Flappy's Buddha?' he asked.

'Buddha?' said Charles. 'I think he's marvellous. In fact, just looking at him inspires me to sit in the Lotus position and reach for Nirvana.'

'Oh, Charles, you are funny!' said Flappy, putting a hand on Gerald's back and leading him towards the door. 'We must begin,' she said.

'Of course.'

'I love everything, Gerald. Send the invoice to Persephone and she'll arrange for the payment of the deposit. Start at once. I want my little sanctuary ready as soon as possible. In the meantime, Charles and I will put up with it as it is, won't we, Charles?'

Gerald was delighted that Flappy had commissioned the entire project. She hadn't even looked at the costings. He'd add a little on for luck, he thought, as he said goodbye to Charles and Flappy and left the cottage. He walked up the path and on through the gardens and thought how very good-looking Charles was. He focused on his eyes, the colour of green topaz, and on his impossibly handsome smile

171

that made the lines on his cheeks deepen in such an attractive way, and he forgot the strange way he'd made his entrance. If he didn't know Flappy so well, he'd think that she and Charles were more than friends.

'I meant to warn you,' said Flappy, as Charles watched Gerald disappear up the garden.

'That was close,' he said, moving away from the window.

'I'm sorry. I got distracted buying a new dress for your party.'

Charles grinned. 'I'm going to dance with you,' he said, slipping his hands around her waist.

'Will there be dancing?' said Flappy. She'd thought it was just a cocktail party.

'Of course there's dancing. I love dancing. There's dinner too. Hedda loves a party.'

'Oh,' said Flappy, wondering whether she'd bought the right dress for the occasion. 'What's Hedda going to wear?'

Charles shrugged. 'I have no idea. I'm much more interested in what you're going to wear and if it's easy to slip out of.' He raised his eyebrows and smiled suggestively.

Flappy laughed. 'You beast!'

Charles swelled with pleasure. 'You beauty!' Then he swept her into his arms and carried her up the stairs.

Chapter 13

The morning of Hedda and Charles's party Flappy awoke at 5 a.m. in an exceedingly good mood. Her whole body was infused with excitement and enthusiasm, and an unconditional love for the world and everyone in it. She was happy. Blissfully happy.

She opened the curtains. Outside, the gardens – the many *beautiful* gardens at Darnley – were bathed in the still, silent semi-light of dawn. Indeed, she could see a pale pink blush glowing on the horizon as morning began to emerge shyly from beneath night's velvety quilt. How beautiful it was, this magical hour, anticipating the gentle stirring of waking animals and birds; nature's inward breath before the hectic activity of day commences.

Flappy's reverie was interrupted by the rumbling sound of Kenneth's snoring next door. But she was in a good mood. Nothing could dampen the happiness she felt inside. In fact, her heart was like a warm bun in her chest, soft and springy, and she felt only love and affection for her husband, even though he did sound like a pig.

She skipped down to the pool, slipped out of her silk dressing gown and dived naked into the water, slicing through it like a gannet. She glided up the first length in an elegant breaststroke, savouring the sensual feeling of the water wrapping around her body and cooling her loins that burned for Charles's touch. The second length was backstroke, the third front crawl and the final length a less impressive breaststroke because by now she had run out of steam. She dried herself with a towel and padded into the gym. She was too restless to do yoga this morning. Too excited. Too happy. There was only one thing to do and that was to dance naked to The Weather Girls' 'It's Raining Men'. She'd always loved that song and today, with the anticipation of Hedda's party, she was in just the right mood to sing along to it. With her hair going fluffy and her cheeks flushing pink, Flappy pranced about the wooden floor, wriggling her hips and kicking her feet, shaking her shoulders and laughing out loud, wildly, passionately, unleashing the beast. The fiery beast that had, for so long, been hidden in the cold of her deepest unconscious, now at liberty to express itself with all its hunger, delight and zeal. It felt wonderful. In fact, she didn't think she had ever felt this wonderful and it was all thanks to Charles, for giving her a bite of ambrosia and unfettering her true nature.

By the time she joined Kenneth at the breakfast table Flappy was dressed, coiffed and ready for her day. And it was a big day today. She had *lots* of important appointments. After all, she had to look her best for Hedda and Charles's party. It was what was expected. She didn't want to let the people of Badley Compton down by looking anything less that immaculate.

Kenneth studied her and his eyes lingered for a long moment as he tried to work out what was different about her. Her hair was the same, though slightly tousled, her eyes were bright and sparkly, but Flappy's eyes had always been bright and sparkly. Was it something about her skin, perhaps? Could it be possible that she was getting younger, not older? Indeed, there was an agility to her movements that hadn't been there before; a bounce. 'Flappy,' he said as he buttered his toast. 'What's going on?'

Flappy's eyes widened. 'What do you mean? Going on where?'

'With you,' he said and his eyes scrutinized her again.

Flappy swallowed. The heat prickled on the back of her neck. 'I'm not sure I know what you're talking about, darling,' she replied breezily, masking her discomfort.

'You look lovely,' he said and smiled. 'You're the only woman in Badley Compton who seems to be getting younger, not older.'

'Oh *that*,' she exclaimed with relief. Well, she knew about *that*. She laughed and was going to repeat her usual thing about the ugly portrait in the attic, when she realized this was not the moment for a joke. It was the moment for cunning. If there was one thing Flappy was good at, it was knowing when to be shrewd. 'I'm just lucky,' she said, then smiled fondly at her husband. 'Good genes and a happy marriage.'

He patted her hand. 'I backed the right horse, didn't I?' he said with a chuckle.

'So did I,' she replied, although she didn't much like being referred to as a horse.

When Persephone arrived at nine, Flappy was ready with a list of things for her to do. 'Good morning, Persephone,' she trilled cheerfully.

'Good morning, Mrs Scott-Booth,' Persephone replied. 'You have a full diary until lunch. Hair appointment at ten with a manicure and pedicure. You should be out by one-thirty.'

'Good,' said Flappy. 'You can drive me into town. I don't want to have to drive back with wet nails. While you're waiting you can run a few errands for me.' She gave Persephone the list. 'Usual things, no surprises, and you can have a coffee and a cake on me at Big Mary's if you like. My hair tends to take some time. I just have so much of it. Poor David spends hours laboriously painting the highlights. I tip him double. One really should be generous when one can.'

The two of them set off in Flappy's Range Rover, listening to Classic FM. Flappy sighed with pleasure at the sight of the blue sky and feathery white clouds that wafted across it. Hedda would be pleased, she thought. No rain to dampen everyone's spirits. It would be a starry night and a full moon for the last party of the summer. Next year Flappy would make sure that *she* gave the last party of the summer. But for now, she was happy to allow Hedda that privilege, considering she was sleeping with her husband. It was the least she could do, to be generous-spirited to Hedda.

She parked at the kerb and the two women got out. Flappy headed for the hairdresser's, while Persephone continued down the street to make her way through Flappy's shopping list. It was only when she had finished and had time to kill that she went off to Big Mary's to take up Flappy's offer of a cake and a cup of coffee. She wasn't surprised to see Mrs Hitchens, Mrs Armitage, Mrs Hancock and Mrs Tennant sitting at a table with their heads together like a quartet of witches. She smiled, greeting them politely as she passed, and went to stand in line behind a dark-haired young man who was talking to Big Mary while she made his coffee. Her eyes settled onto the cakes and she wondered which she would choose today. Would it be the one with sprinkles or the sticky one with pink icing? The man turned to her as Big Mary took a plate down from the shelf behind her. He caught Persephone's eye and smiled. 'Hello,' he said.

'Hi,' Persephone replied.

The man liked what he saw, for he added, 'I like the chocolate cake the best. I had a slice yesterday and I dreamed about it all night.'

Persephone laughed. 'I'm more of a vanilla girl myself. I can't decide which one to go for.'

'What's the choice?' he asked, joining her in looking through the glass. Persephone pointed at the two cakes.

He thought about it for a moment, scratching his chin. 'Personally, I'd go for sprinkles.'

'Why?'

'Because they remind me of my childhood. I'm a nostalgic person,' he said with an apologetic smile, as if being nostalgic was a flaw. Persephone noticed that his eyes were green, like sea glass.

'Okay, I'll go for sprinkles,' she said. 'I'm nostalgic too.'

'Don't blame me if you regret it.'

'I won't regret it,' she laughed. 'I think it's a good choice.'

'My name's George, by the way.' He extended his hand.

'Persephone,' she replied, shaking it.

'Are you from round here?'

'Yes, I live in Badley Compton.'

'Nice place, isn't it?'

'I like it. Too quiet for some people, I imagine.' He looked like a Londoner. Certainly not from down here in Devon, she thought. Badley Compton hadn't produced anything as attractive, as far as she knew.

'Anyway, better be going. It was nice meeting you,' he said, taking his coffee cup off the counter.

'Thanks for the cake advice,' she said, disappointed that he was leaving.

'Pleasure. I hope you enjoy it.'

Persephone asked Big Mary for a caffè latte and a cake. When she turned round, George had gone.

Sometime later, a few blocks up the road, Flappy was sitting in a comfortable chair in front of the mirror, reading *Hello!* magazine, when Mabel walked in. Behind her, the hairdresser was carefully painting strands of her hair and wrapping them in foil.

'Hello, Flappy,' said Mabel, surprised to see Flappy reading that sort of magazine.

Flappy smiled. 'Hello, Mabel. Are you coming to have your hair done?'

'I am,' said Mabel cheerfully. 'I'm excited about the party tonight. Big Mary says there's a surprise entertainment.'

'Oh,' said Flappy, trying not to look put out. It was usually Flappy who arranged parties with entertainers in Badley Compton. 'How thrilling. I wonder who she's got.'

'I've got no idea. Big Mary didn't say. I'm sure it'll be something exciting.'

Mabel settled into the chair beside Flappy. 'Do you want to read this?' said Flappy, handing her the magazine. 'I've read it. I love reading *Hello!* at the hairdresser's, don't you? One gets so weary of reading the *Economist* and the *Spectator* all the time. It's good to give one's brain a rest.'

Mabel, who felt no shame in reading *Hello!*, took it. 'By the by, guess who I saw being chatted up in Big Mary's?'

Flappy couldn't be bothered to guess. After all, it could be just about anyone. 'I don't know,' she replied. 'Who?'

'Persephone,' Mabel told her with glee.

'Well, that doesn't surprise me. She's a pretty girl.'

'But you won't believe who was chatting her up.'

'Who?' Flappy asked.

'Hedda and Charles's son, George.'

Now she'd got Flappy's interest. 'Hedda and Charles's son is in Badley Compton?' asked Flappy in surprise. She vaguely knew they had children, but they hadn't mentioned that any of them were coming to the party.

'Yes. He's very handsome with his father's eyes,' said Mabel. 'Charles has such beautiful eyes, doesn't he?'

179

'I'm not sure I've noticed,' said Flappy coolly. 'Tell me, did they exchange numbers? Did they have coffee together?'

'No, they chatted about the cakes. He asked her if she was from Badley Compton and then he left with his takeaway coffee. I think he fancied her though. It was all in the body language and in his lingering longer than he needed to.' Mabel enjoyed giving Flappy the details and was delighted that she was devouring them.

'Did he indeed,' Flappy murmured thoughtfully. She narrowed her eyes and made space in her busy mind for an idea. Sure enough, in one popped and it was, it must be acknowledged, an exceedingly good one.

Mabel watched her with interest. She knew Flappy well enough to know what the focused and alert expression on her face meant. 'What are you plotting?' she asked.

Flappy took her phone out of her handbag. 'I'm going to get Persephone invited to the party tonight.'

Mabel looked horrified. 'You're not going to ask Hedda, are you?'

'Of course I'm not going to ask Hedda,' said Flappy. 'I'm much too subtle for that.'

'How are you going to do it?'

'Listen and learn, Mabel,' she said with a smile. 'Persephone needs a boyfriend and George is just the sort of man she deserves. His great-uncle was a marquess, after all.' A moment later Persephone answered the phone. 'Persephone,' said Flappy. 'I need you to do me a teeny favour. Go to the florist on Branwell Street and buy a generous bouquet of flowers for Hedda. Whites and greens only, please. It must be elegant and tasteful and very big. Cynthia knows what I like and I have an account there, so you won't need to pay. I'd like you to write a note to go with them, saying, "Darling Hedda, wishing you luck for tonight, with love Flappy." Then I want you to drive to Compton Court and deliver them. It's important that you don't give them to Johnson. Do you understand? I need you to hand them *personally* to Hedda. You must insist. Then, you're to ask her if you can help in any way. I want you to offer your services. I doubt very much she'll need them, but it's nice to offer, isn't it?'

When she hung up, Mabel frowned. 'How can you guarantee that Hedda will invite her to her party?'

Flappy gave her knowing smile. If Flappy was good at one thing, it was understanding people. 'She will,' she replied with certainty. 'Because that's the sort of person Hedda is. Besides, she's invited most of the town already and she will want a pretty girl to entertain her son. I guarantee you, my dear Mabel, that Persephone will be coming to the party tonight and she'll have the perfect dress to wear.' Flappy folded her hands in her lap and smiled at her reflection, feeling very pleased with herself.

An hour later Persephone stood in front of the big door of Compton Court and rang the bell. In her arms she cradled an enormous bouquet of arum lilies and white roses, just as Flappy had requested. It was a beautiful bouquet and must have cost a fortune. It wasn't long before the door opened and Johnson stood before her, a quizzical look on his face.

He was about to instruct her to take her delivery to the tradesman's entrance at the back of the house where the various people hired for the party were busy unpacking their goods, but he recognized Mrs Scott-Booth's car and realized suddenly that the girl with the flowers was the PA he had spoken to on the phone on various occasions. 'You must be Persephone,' he said.

Persephone smiled. 'And you must be Johnson,' she replied.

'I am indeed. Shall I take those for you?' He reached out for the flowers.

'Mrs Scott-Booth has specifically requested that I deliver them personally to Mrs Harvey-Smith.'

Johnson raised his eyebrows. This was very unusual. 'Did she now?' he said, reflecting on the redoubtable Mrs Scott-Booth.

'If you wouldn't mind, I'd better do as she asks,' said Persephone. 'She doesn't take well to being disobeyed.'

Johnson raised his fluffy white eyebrows and nodded, a knowing and sympathetic look on his face. 'Then you'd better come in. Mrs Harvey-Smith is in the marquee. I'm sure she won't mind giving you a moment of her time.'

Persephone followed Johnson through the house to the lawn at the back where a beautiful Indian style marquee in reds and blues and golds had been erected on the grass. It was the most splendid marquee Persephone had ever seen. She wondered what Flappy would think of it, because, as far as she knew, Flappy had never put up a marquee of such splendour and would, no doubt, feel a little put out. In and out of this marquee came a stream of busy people, carrying chairs and tables, vases and flowers, lighting equipment and goodness knows what else, like bees in a hive they were, and in the middle of the marquee, talking to an efficient and important-looking woman, was the queen bee herself, Hedda Harvey-Smith, casual in a pair of jeans and polo shirt.

Johnson and Persephone made their way across the floor. Hedda broke off her conversation. When she saw Persephone and the flowers, she smiled. 'Are they for me?' she asked, delight lighting up her face, even though there was already a magnificent display of flowers on each table.

'I'm Persephone, Mrs—' she began.

'Flappy's PA!' Hedda exclaimed. 'I've heard so much about you. What a darling you are to bring me flowers. How kind and sweet of Flappy.' She read the note. 'Typical,' she said, shaking her head with affection. 'Will you thank her very much. I'm touched that she should think of it.'

'Mrs Scott-Booth asked me to ask you whether you needed any help.' Persephone laughed. 'But I can see that you already have everything under control. The marquee is amazing. I've never seen such a beautiful marquee in my life.'

'I'm so happy you like it. Nothing to do with me, though, and everything to do with Jill here. Jill, this is Persephone.' The two women shook hands.

Johnson took the flowers from Persephone. 'I'll go and put these in a vase,' he said and set off in the direction of the house.

Then Hedda's gaze strayed over Persephone's shoulder and a look of adoration came over her face. 'George!' she gushed.

Persephone turned to see the young man she'd been

talking to in the café that morning. He looked pleasantly surprised to see her. 'Persephone?' he exclaimed, his smile broadening.

Hedda was confused. 'You two know each other?'

'We met at Mary's this morning,' he told her. 'Did you enjoy your sprinkly cake?'

Persephone laughed. 'I did,' she replied.

'Phew! I thought you were here to berate me for choosing the wrong one.'

Hedda narrowed her eyes and looked from Persephone to her son and back again. 'Actually, Persephone,' she began, 'I really could do with your help. George is going to put out the place cards. Perhaps you could give him a hand. And, while you're doing it, perhaps you might like to write one for yourself. I'd love you to come tonight, if you're free. You can sit next to George.'

Persephone had not expected this. She felt like Cinderella being invited to the ball. 'Oh, I'd love to,' she replied. 'If you're sure I won't muck up your placement.'

Hedda touched her arm and smiled. 'My dear, you'll be the only person of George's age. I think it's more a case of *us* needing *you*.'

'Come on, Persephone,' said George. 'Let's put you to work.'

Persephone was waiting outside the hairdresser's in Flappy's car when Flappy's appointment came to an end at half past one. Flappy came out of the building with her fingers splayed, the crimson paint not quite dry on her nails.

Persephone opened the door for her and helped her with the seat belt. It would not do to smudge her polish. Smudged polish was very common. As Persephone set off for Darnley, she told Flappy about Hedda's invitation.

'How nice of her,' said Flappy, feigning ignorance. 'What's this son of hers like? Is he handsome?'

'*I* think he is,' Persephone replied. 'But beauty is in the eye of the beholder, isn't it?'

'It is indeed,' said Flappy. She could tell that Persephone was taken with him. After all, Flappy had an acute understanding of people. 'Isn't it lucky you have a lovely new dress to wear,' she added.

Persephone was truly grateful for that. 'I can't thank you enough, Mrs Scott-Booth, for buying it for me. It's like you knew I'd be invited to the party.'

Flappy gave a secretive little smile. 'Let's just say, Persephone, that I had a sixth sense you might be needing a dress.'

Persephone shook her head in wonder. 'You must be psychic,' she mused.

'Not psychic,' Flappy corrected. 'Just intuitive. It must be all the meditation I'm doing.'

Chapter 14

Flappy stood in front of the long mirror in her bedroom and admired her reflection. It could not be denied, blue really was her colour. She smiled with satisfaction, and a little sadness too, because as she got older she felt more keenly the passing of time. She saw it too, in the lines deepening on her face and in the texture of her skin which was no longer youthful. This loss of bloom was not an easy thing for a beautiful woman to accept – the thought that one day people would refer to her beauty in the past tense, when all her life she'd been told how very lovely she was. She did not want to be told she *used to be lovely, once.* Ugly people fared better, she decided, turning to admire herself from the side, for they had nothing to lose and everything to gain, as old age evened the playing field. Well, the playing field was far from even and Flappy still looked good. Exceedingly good. At least, she reassured herself, she had a lively and interesting personality, because time could not rob her of that. As long as she had all her marbles, she'd continue to dazzle with her witty repartee and intelligent conversation. She'd still be an asset at any dining table.

Kenneth wandered into her bedroom in black tie, which Flappy had insisted he wear even though the invitation had stated simply 'glamorous'. If Flappy was going to wear a floor-length gown, Kenneth had to be dressed to match. She smiled at him fondly. He might look like a toad but he made a fine-looking toad in black tie. Kenneth admired his wife. 'You look stunning, darling,' he said and Flappy shrugged off the compliment as if it embarrassed her, which it didn't. Compliments never did.

'Oh, darling, you're too sweet,' she said. 'One has to work hard at my age to be halfway decent. But thank you. You look handsome too.'

Kenneth fiddled with his waistband. 'The trousers are a little tight around the belly,' he said with a chortle. 'But I think I'll get through the evening without bursting out of them.'

Flappy didn't like the thought of Kenneth bursting out of his trousers. 'Have you practised sitting down?' she asked. It would be awful if he sat down and popped the button.

Kenneth plonked himself down on her bed with a wince.

'Suck it in, Kenneth,' said Flappy. 'We girls have to suck in our stomachs all the time.' Which wasn't true, because Flappy's stomach was perfectly flat.

Kenneth sucked his in, but this did nothing to ease the discomfort and only turned his face the colour of claret. Then Flappy had an idea. 'Whip them off, darling,' she ordered. 'I'm going to sew a piece of elastic into them, then you don't have to use the button at all.' She went to her sewing basket, which she rarely opened because there was usually someone around to do any sewing for her, and pulled out a needle, a reel of cotton and a packet of black elastic. Five minutes later Kenneth was pulling the trousers back over his hips and settling them onto his waist with satisfaction. 'Much better,' he exclaimed, sitting on the edge of her bed once more and bouncing a little to show how much better they really were.

'Don't forget to do up the flies,' she warned. 'We don't want anything falling out, do we?'

'Old birds don't fall out of their nests,' said Kenneth with a grin.

'That's disgusting, Kenneth. I don't want to think about old birds at all!'

But Kenneth chuckled in his good-natured way and went to kiss her on the cheek. 'Thank you, Flappy. I don't know what I'd do without you. You're a gem. A real gem. A diamond. The best gem there is.'

Flappy smiled back, the knot of guilt tightening just beneath her ribs. It was unforgivable really, to betray Kenneth in this way, she thought, considering what a nice, sweet man he was. If he'd been horrid, he'd deserve it. But he did not deserve to be a cuckold. However, there was nothing she could do about it, since neither she nor Charles was going to end the affair. She would simply have to accept that this was the way things were and not worry about the future, or indeed, what she'd got up to in the past. She had to live in the moment. If Flappy was good at one thing, it was living in the moment when living in the moment was required.

The two of them set off in Kenneth's Jaguar. Flappy looked out of the window and felt a sudden wave of melancholy. The early autumn light was tender, bathing the rolling fields of stubble in a soft amber glow. The sky was a duck egg blue, the first star twinkling like the light of a distant ship shining through mist. A full moon was beginning to rise even as the sun sunk slowly behind the trees. The seasons were at their loveliest when one gave way to the other. It was the change that was so enchanting. Flappy felt that change now, as they drove down the winding lanes towards Compton Court. There was a dampness in the air that hadn't been there before, a sweet smell of nature on the turn. The slow dying of summer.

The lights of Compton Court were ablaze. Flares lit up the drive and fairy lights glittered in the trees. Flappy was too stunned by the beauty of it to be jealous. Besides, she was going to have a wonderful evening; jealousy had no place in the evening that Flappy had envisaged for herself.

Guests were directed by the Compton Court gardeners to park in a field not far from the house. As Kenneth drove into his given slot, Flappy's eyes swept keenly over the familiar faces of those making their way up a path, which cut through the long grasses to the house. Luckily, Flappy was not wearing high heels. She spotted Sally leaning heavily on her husband's arm as she tottered unsteadily on vertiginous stilettos. When Flappy got out of the car, she put her delicate silk shoes onto the grass and, lifting the front of her dress slightly, giving a glimpse of her slender ankles, she walked easily and elegantly towards the party. Once at the house, whose façade, it had to be acknowledged, was one of the most beautiful Flappy had ever seen, she and Kenneth were directed along a pathway of flares to the back of the house where the marquee stood in all its Indian magnificence. Flappy was spellbound. She had never seen a marquee like it. Really, it was the sort of wonder one might find in the gardens of the Maharaja's Palace in Udaipur – not that she'd ever been there. Hedda and Charles were at the entrance, with their four children, one of whom Flappy assumed must be George.

'Hedda!' exclaimed Flappy, taking her hands and kissing her cheeks.

'Flappy!' exclaimed Hedda, running her eyes over Flappy's dress with admiration. 'You look gorgeous,' she said.

'So do you,' Flappy replied, although, if she were being honest, 'gorgeous' was not the appropriate word for Hedda. She was nicely dressed in a long purple gown, which, Flappy conceded, was a good colour against her pale English skin and brown hair, but she was much too stocky to ever be considered gorgeous. However, what she lacked in gorgeousness was made up for in a vivacious and confident personality – and in the diamonds and amethysts sparkling at her ears and throat. Family heirlooms passed down from the marchioness, no doubt.

When Flappy saw Charles, she sank into those sea-green eyes and felt herself swelling with joy. Tonight was going to be special, she knew. Tonight they would dance and stroll around the garden in moonlight and no one would know the deliciously wicked things they had done in the cottage. 'Flappy,' said Charles, taking her in in one greedy sweep of his eyes. 'You look magnificent.'

Charles, who was in black tie like Kenneth, wore it well.

Flappy knew there was no elastic beneath *his* jacket on account of drinking too many bottles of claret. His hair was brushed off his face, revealing a Hollywood style widow's peak, and his white teeth gleamed against his tanned skin. She caught her breath and smiled, because she knew if she opened her mouth she'd say something that would give her away. If Flappy knew one thing, it was when to keep her mouth *shut*.

Flappy moved on to greet the children. They were nice-looking, smiley people with their father's good teeth and their mother's good skin. George was the most handsome, Flappy thought with satisfaction, and she wondered whether Persephone had arrived and already dazzled him in her dress.

Kenneth and Flappy walked on into the marquee, accepting glasses of champagne and greeting friends as they made their way through. Flappy was astonished by the decorations. The elaborate displays of flowers on the tables, the tiny ceiling lights that looked like stars, the pillars that appeared to be made out of roses. Flappy couldn't help but calculate the amount of money that must have been spent on this lavish event and realized, with growing admiration, that Hedda and Charles were a lot richer than she had previously suspected.

'Flappy!' called Mabel, waving as she made her way to her through the throng. 'Isn't this divine!' she gushed when she reached her. The two women kissed. 'It must have cost a fortune!'

Flappy looked disapproving. 'Oh, Mabel, it's frightfully common to talk about money at the best of times, but on a night like this. Really, I would never *ever* start estimating the cost of a party while I was at it.'

Mabel's smile faltered. 'You're absolutely right, Flappy. I don't know what's got into me. But isn't it spectacular!'

'It really is,' said Flappy. 'And you look lovely, Mabel.'

Mabel's smile returned. She'd bought the dress at Chic Boutique. Cheryl had told her what Flappy had bought so Mabel could buy something similar but not *too* similar. 'Isn't it fun to dress up? I haven't dressed up like this in so long. In fact, I don't think Badley Compton has ever seen such an extravaganza!'

Her comment hit a nerve, and Flappy had been determined that tonight of all nights nerves were *not* going to be hit. However, after all the parties Flappy had hosted over the years, the cocktail parties and dinner parties and charity fund-raising parties, it was galling to be told that Hedda's party outshone them all. Flappy had to dig deep to find her patience, but find it she did. 'You're quite right, Mabel. I don't think Badley Compton has ever witnessed something on this scale. How lucky we all are that Hedda and Charles decided to move *here*, to our little provincial corner of the world.'

Mabel was suddenly aware of her faux pas. But how like Flappy to be so generous-spirited, she thought. 'I might add, Flappy, that although this marquee is bigger than anything I've seen at Darnley, there's a classiness to your parties that is unique to *you*. Not even Hedda with all her millions and squillions can outshine you in that department.'

Flappy lifted her chin. She knew that what Mabel said was

not strictly true. After all, Hedda was the niece of a marquess: if anyone knew about class it was her. However, in Mabel's eyes at least, Flappy's *amour propre* was restored, for it was true, Flappy's parties did have a certain magic.

It wasn't long before Sally tottered over in a lather of excitement. 'Flappy, Mabel, guess who's arrived?' she asked.

Flappy didn't like guessing games. Flappy liked to *know*. 'Just about everyone in Badley Compton,' she answered with a dry smile.

'Monty Don,' said Mabel, her face opening into a beaming smile.

'Yes! Monty Don!' Sally squealed. 'He's even more handsome in real life than he is on the telly.'

Flappy felt a little frisson of interest. However she did not want Sally to know that she was impressed. Flappy was not a crowd follower under any circumstances. Her natural habitat was in front of the crowd, leading it, setting it an example, *always* ahead of it. 'I'm not very interested in his looks,' she said with a sniff. 'But I cannot deny he is a wonderful horticulturalist. I would very much like the opportunity to discuss *The Irvington Diaries* with him.'

'I just want to meet him!' said Sally, roaring with laughter. 'I don't care what he talks about.'

A moment later Esther and Madge came over to add their enthusiasm to Sally's, but Flappy's attention was elsewhere. As she drifted off in search of Charles, her friends watched her go in puzzlement. 'Too much meditation is a bad thing,' said Esther darkly. 'I've always thought it highly overrated.'

'She's just on another plane,' said Madge. 'Any woman

of our age who doesn't get excited about Monty Don is on another plane.'

Sally nodded. 'To be frank, we have more chance of talking to Monty Don if Flappy is not with us. Flappy will only dominate. You know what she's like,' she added, aware that it was not acceptable to be rude about Flappy. 'She's much too beautiful.'

'Well, come on then, girls. Let's go and find him,' said Mabel, setting off into the crowd followed by Esther, Madge and Sally.

Flappy got caught by the vicar and his wife before she had a chance to find Charles. Being the polite and gracious woman she was, and Flappy was, indeed, enormously polite and gracious, she did not extricate herself, which would have been rude, but engaged in conversation with them as if the words they said were the most interesting she had heard all week. When she finally did manage to move on, she heard the Reverend turn to his wife and say, 'She's delightful, isn't she, Joan. Always has time for everyone.' Flappy felt better about her infidelity at that point, because the vicar had God's ear and she knew she was a teeny bit in arrears there.

Before she could get to Charles, she was detained by countless people, which was very annoying. But that was the trouble with going to a party where one knew everyone, it meant that everyone wanted to talk to one. By the time Flappy managed to get close to him, the room fell silent in response to a gong and they were summoned to dinner. This was not what she had planned for herself this evening. But she swallowed her disappointment, smiled as if she was having the most marvellous time and went to look at the seating plan. There would be opportunities later, she knew, to talk to Charles. She'd dance with him, for sure, and walk with him in the garden with the twinkling fairy lights on the trees and the full moon above, and it would be romantic and tender and sensual. Perhaps they'd steal a kiss in a secret corner of the garden. She knew there would be many secret gardens, as there were at Darnley. Indeed, Darnley had the most beautiful secret gardens in the whole of Badley Compton.

As Flappy stood by the big board that displayed the seating plan, Kenneth sidled up beside her. 'Hello, darling,' he said, slipping a hand beneath her arm. 'Found where you're sitting yet?'

'No, you?'

'Yes, I'm at Hedda's table,' he told her.

'And I'm not?' Flappy's heart sank. Surely, being such a close friend of Hedda's she should be sitting at her table. Flappy did not know how she would live it down if her friends saw that she was not on Top Table.

'You're next to Charles,' said Kenneth, squeezing her arm. He more than anyone knew how much it meant to Flappy to be seated next to the host.

Flappy's spirits sprang back to life with a jolt. 'Ah, next to the host. What an honour,' she said, barely able to contain her excitement.

'Where are you sitting, Flappy?' It was Mabel and the others who had yet to find Monty Don.

'I'm sitting next to the host,' Flappy replied with a sniff.

'I'm so *so* lucky to have such a good placement.' The four women looked at her with envy, because second to Monty Don, they'd like to be seated next to Charles Harvey-Smith.

Flappy could not get to the table quick enough. Anyone who tried to detain her was told, in a very polite and gracious way, of course, that she must hurry to her seat because she was next to the host, and everyone understood that it was impolite to keep the host waiting. At last, she and Charles stood side by side. He looked down at her with his impossibly beautiful eyes and Flappy sank into them as if she were the Little Mermaid being swallowed by the sea. 'Hedda did the placement,' he said with a smile that made Flappy's stomach fizz.

'How nice of her,' Flappy replied. *And naïve*, she thought a little smugly.

Charles pulled out her chair and she sat down. She greeted the man on her right, who she'd never met before. He looked like an old professor with small round glasses and thinning hair. He introduced himself but Flappy was too distracted to catch his name. She noticed that, on the other side of Charles, was the insipid, though fearfully-good-at-bridge, Amanda Worthington. There was no competition there, she thought as she flicked out her napkin and laid it across her knees. Charles filled her wine glass and Flappy took a sip. As she was on his right, she had him to herself for the first half of dinner. He'd have to turn and talk to Amanda for the second half. However, Flappy knew there was a very strong chance he wouldn't turn at all. When not at the bridge table, Amanda had little to say.

Charles pressed his knee against hers. She pressed it back. As they talked, he managed to steal his hand onto her thigh. 'You're wearing a beautiful dress, Flappy,' he whispered. 'But all I can think of is peeling it off.'

'Oh, Beastie, how naughty of you to say that here!'

'But it's all I can think of, Beauty. Aren't I lucky not only to be seated next to the most beautiful woman in the room, but to be sleeping with her as well.'

Flappy's eyes slid to her left and right. No one was listening. Each person at the table was engrossed in their own conversation. 'You're getting reckless, Beastie. I'm going to have to tell you to calm down.'

'And I'm going to have to tell you that I can't and that I won't. You do things to me, Flappy, that no other woman does. I think we can escape after dinner so that I can do things to *you* that no other man does.'

Flappy was beginning to get a little hot. She could feel her face burning. He squeezed her thigh. 'I'm going to dance with you tonight, Flappy, and then I'm going to make love to you.'

With that to look forward to, Flappy took a gulp of wine. Then another. She needed fortification to get through dinner when really she wanted to run into the house and lie down on one of Hedda's four-poster beds, and have Charles slip off her dress and the silk panties she was wearing especially and do all manner of delicious things to her. It was almost too much to bear. But bear it she did, because if there was one thing Flappy was good at, it was restraining the beast when the beast needed to be restrained.

197

As it happened, Charles did turn. Much to Flappy's annoyance, because it meant that she had to talk to the professor. Her gaze strayed through the tables to Persephone. Flappy was pleased to see that her PA was in her lovely new dress, sitting next to none other than George. She felt very pleased with herself. Wasn't it thrilling when a plan came together?

All the while she listened to the professor, Charles kept refilling her glass of wine. Flappy's smile was set upon her face as if in aspic, and the professor kept talking, unaware that he was boring his beautiful companion. Goodness, he was dull. In fact, Flappy couldn't remember the last time she had sat next to someone whose tone of voice sent her to sleep. She couldn't wait for dinner to be over so that she and Charles could escape.

Flappy's ordeal came to an end when Charles tapped his knife against his wine glass and the conversations in the room slowly died away. He stood up. *How tall and handsome he looks*, thought Flappy, gazing up at him in wonder. 'My dear friends,' he began, and she could tell that he'd once walked the boards because his deep and booming voice reminded her of those great actors of the Royal Shakespeare Company. *He'd make a wonderful Hamlet*, she thought as her mind drifted once again to the four-poster bed and the fun they were going to have in it. 'Hedda and I are delighted that you are all here tonight because we really wanted to meet you and to thank you for welcoming us to Badley Compton so warmly. When Hedda suggested we move here I wasn't very enthusiastic, but we drove down and she showed me the house, which was lovely, of course, but it was the town that swung it for me. Everyone greeted me, everyone smiled, everyone had time. How different it was from London where no one has time for anyone. The Scott-Booth Golf Club might have been a key factor in my decision-making, of course ... ' He laughed and the room laughed with him. Flappy was thrilled that her name had been mentioned. 'What I want to say is, thank you for being such a charming community of which Hedda and I are honoured to be a part. I raise my glass to my lovely wife, for arranging this evening so beautifully. I have to admit, I had nothing to do with it. And I raise my glass to you, the people of Badley Compton, our new friends.' The room got to their feet and toasted Hedda and the people of Badley Compton. Flappy clinked her glass against Charles's and he gave her a smile that held within it all the naughty things they had ever done. Flappy's cheeks flushed with pleasure for that smile was for her and her alone. Never before in Flappy's life had she felt so singled out and special.

Suddenly, the music started. It was a tango. If Flappy knew one thing, it was how to dance the tango.

Chapter 15

Flappy was a little unsteady on her feet. The wine and the excitement had gone to her head and she felt dizzy and giggly and a teeny bit reckless. Years ago, when Flappy was a young woman, she had worked in Buenos Aires as an au pair. This was not something she ever spoke of, because being an au pair was not the kind of thing she would have liked any of her friends to know she had been. However, been it she had, and during that time she had fallen in love with the tango. She'd sit on the cobbled streets of San Telmo, the oldest part of the city, and watch the Porteños (the correct word for 'people of Buenos Aires') dance. The tango was so full of passion that it had, perhaps, resonated with the deep, concealed passion inside of her, which yearned for release. After a while, one of the dancers, an elderly man with a comic moustache and eyebrows that danced a tango of their own, asked her if she'd like to learn, and she had jumped at the opportunity. Now, as she walked unsteadily onto the dance floor with Charles, Flappy was keen to show off her moves, if she could remember them. Naturally, one needs a partner who knows those moves too, and Charles didn't. This, however, did not deter Flappy. Fortified by wine, she was in no mind to be deterred.

There were few people on the dance floor but Flappy was aware that she held every eye in the room. That in itself was intoxicating: she did like to be the centre of attention. Charles pulled her into his arms and they did what every ignorant, wannabe tango dancer does: they marched in a line, cheek to cheek. But Flappy was not an ignorant, wannabe tango dancer. She was the real thing and she was going to show it. With a theatrical gesture, as if she were on stage at Señor Tango in Buenos Aires, she pushed herself away from Charles and deftly, and quite unexpectedly, broke into a sequence of complicated steps that came back to her as if they were innately part of her. Carrying her on a wave of nostalgia, the music took her back to San Telmo. She pointed her toes and dragged them, she made the figure of eight and then reversed it. She kicked her legs and strutted and stamped, and she was unaware of the mesmerized guests getting up from their chairs one by one so they could see her better. Flappy moved across the dance floor with the elegance and poise of a professional dancer and reunited with Charles, who was as astonished as everyone else in the room, not least Kenneth, who had no idea his wife could dance the tango. Charles did not have to do much, for Flappy danced around him, running her feet up his legs and through them, and arching her back and tossing her head. When the music ended, she lay back in Charles's arms and kicked her leg in the air. The skirt of her dress floated away, revealing slim thighs and graceful calves. They held this position for a long moment, because Flappy was aware of how good it looked. Charles was grateful at this point to have something important to do. The room erupted into applause. Flappy felt as if she were going to burst with pleasure, and probably exhaustion too, because now it was over she realized she was a teeny bit out of breath and had possibly overdone it.

Flappy stood up. Charles kissed her hand. Then he turned to the guests and gesticulated at Flappy, which was her cue to curtsey. She wasn't sure her legs would manage a curtsey, so she bowed instead and everyone cheered. Flappy felt like a star, which was a very good feeling indeed. She blew kisses as if she were on stage and beamed a triumphant smile. Charles turned to her and shook his head in wonder. 'Where did you learn to dance the tango?' he asked.

'Buenos Aires,' she replied.

'What were you doing in Buenos Aires?'

This was one of those moments when Flappy had the choice between the truth, which was discomforting, and a lie, which was beneath her. Without hesitation, she chose the latter. 'My father worked at the British Embassy in Buenos Aires. Tango was one of the many things I learned there.'

'You're a dark horse, Flappy,' he said, leading her off the dance floor. 'I suppose you're going to tell me you learned to play polo next!'

Before Flappy could reply, she was being congratulated by her friends. Then Hedda was rushing up and throwing her arms around her and saying she had never seen anything so wonderful in her whole life. 'You're so full of surprises,

Flappy. I needn't have bothered with the entertainment,' she laughed.

Flappy and Charles went back to their seats and the lights dimmed. A shiny black piano sat in a beam of light. Flappy wondered who was going to play it. She couldn't imagine anyone could be more entertaining than her. However, there had been many moments in her life when she'd had to admit that she was wrong, and this was another one. To rapturous applause, Jason Donovan walked onto the dance floor.

Flappy was amazed that Hedda had managed to get Jason Donovan to come and sing at her party. She really must be infinitely richer than previously thought. Under normal circumstances, Flappy might have been a teeny bit jealous, but tonight, after having danced the tango with such success, she felt only elation. She took a gulp of wine from the glass Charles had just refreshed, and listened to Jason's wonderfully deep and warm voice singing all her favourite songs. As she sat back in her chair and let the music entertain her, she reflected on the evening and how it was possibly the most thrilling evening she had ever had. Charles pressed his knee against hers and she knew it was only going to get better.

It was nearly midnight when Charles and Flappy escaped into the garden. Hedda was on the dance floor with her children, their partners, and George and Persephone, who had eyes only for each other, but Flappy was too busy to notice the success of her endeavours. She was following Charles out into the night, through a door in a wall and on into a secret garden, eerily silver in the watery light of the moon. He swung her round and kissed her. 'You were wonderful on the dance floor, Beauty. I don't think I'll forget tonight for as long as I live.'

'Oh, Beastie, you're too sweet,' she replied.

'And you're too modest.'

'I know, it's one of my many faults. I must learn to accept compliments when someone is kind enough to give them.'

'I want to shower you in compliments,' he murmured, pressing his lips to her temple. 'But I'm going to shower you in kisses instead.' Flappy was in heaven. In fact, she didn't think heaven would be anything like as lovely as this. 'I love you, Flappy,' said Charles.

Flappy was taken aback. Love was a very powerful word. In fact, Flappy had only ever said 'I love you' to Kenneth and that was a very long time ago. She didn't have time to reflect on love right now, but she knew she must still love Kenneth all the same. She wasn't sure, however, that she loved Charles.

Charles's lips were poised above hers and he was gazing into her eyes expectantly. Naturally, he wanted to hear that she loved him too. At this point, Flappy had the choice to tell him the truth, which was that she *lusted* after him, or to lie and tell him that she *loved* him. Flappy did neither. She pulled his head down and gave him a long and passionate kiss.

A loud gasp cut through the moment and brought the two of them back to reality with a terrible thud. They sprang apart as if stung. There, in the entrance to the walled garden, were Persephone and George.

Flappy stared at them in horror. So many terrifying visions passed in front of her eyes: Kenneth's despair, Hedda's fury, Badley Compton shunning her as a harlot and a slut. She wished the ground would open, swallow her whole and never let her out again, ever. This was possibly the worst moment of her life.

'Come now, George,' said Charles in a tone of voice designed to make light of the situation.

George stared at his father in disgust. 'What are you doing, Dad?' he exclaimed.

'I was kissing Flappy. I admit it. Guilty as charged. But it's one little kiss.' He grinned at Flappy. 'We're both a bit drunk, aren't we, Flappy?'

Flappy barely dared look at Persephone, but she could see, in her peripheral vision, that the girl was shocked. In fact, her face had gone white and she looked almost ghostly in the moonlight. Flappy did not know what to do. Flappy, who always knew the right thing to say, had no words. Flappy, who was usually so in control, found, to her utter dismay, that she had none.

Then Persephone spoke. 'Mrs Scott-Booth. I believe the doctor told you not to drink alcohol with your medication.'

Flappy leapt at the chance to deny responsibility. 'I *have* been drinking,' she said in a confused voice, which she thought might help convince George that she was not in her right mind. She looked at Charles. 'I'm sorry. I'm not sure what I'm doing. I think I'd better go home.'

'I'll drive you,' said Persephone, stepping forward to lend an arm. 'Lean on me.' Then to George, 'I'm sorry, George. But I think I'd better see Mrs Scott-Booth home. She's clearly not well. Darnley's only ten minutes away. I'll come straight back.'

George gave her a wan smile and scratched his head. It was clear that he found the situation bewildering. 'You're very kind, Persephone.' Then to Charles, 'We need to talk. Mum is not going to be at all happy when she hears about this.'

Flappy fled through the door in the wall, the threat of Hedda hearing about it ringing in her ears. Suddenly she wanted to be as far away from Compton Court as possible.

Persephone managed to get Flappy into her car without anyone seeing her, thanks to having helped George with the placement the day before and consequently knowing her way to the car park without having to go through the marquee. Once on their way, Flappy confessed. 'I'm going to tell you the truth, Persephone,' she said with a sigh. If Flappy was good at one thing, it was knowing when the game was over and it was time to be honest. 'You managed to get me out of there with dignity, for which I am enormously grateful.' She hesitated, because what she was about to say had precious little dignity in it. 'I've been having an affair with Charles. It's been going on for about three weeks. I lost control.'

Persephone stared at the road ahead, which was a relief for Flappy, because she did not want her to crash the car nor did she want to look her in the eye. 'I would never judge you, Mrs Scott-Booth,' Persephone said calmly. 'I know very little about your life. I'm in no position to pass judgement.'

'I think you'd better call me Flappy,' said Flappy. 'If we're going to be discussing my sex life, you'd better consider yourself a friend.'

Persephone smiled sympathetically. 'You're not the first to

have had an affair and got caught, Flappy. What you need to do now is limit the damage. The two people most concerned are Mr Scott-Booth and Mrs Harvey-Smith.'

'If you're suggesting I tell Kenneth, I'm afraid I simply cannot. It will break his heart. I can't do that to him.' The thought of losing Kenneth caused Flappy's heart to twist with pain. She put an unsteady hand on her bosom. 'I love Kenneth,' she said in a small voice. 'I don't love Charles. It's just an infatuation. A foolish infatuation.'

'It's not foolish, Flappy. It's understandable. He's very handsome. I'm not surprised you fell for his charm.'

'You're very kind, Persephone, but at my age I should know how to behave.'

'Age has nothing to do with it. You're as old as you feel, and why should a sixty something-year-old have fewer sexual feelings than a twenty-year-old. You're a human being who's attracted to another. It's as simple as that.'

'But I'm married, and happily married too. I got carried away. Do you think George will tell his mother?'

Persephone, who had only known George for two days, could not answer that. 'I'll find out for you and let you know. If he does tell his mother I suggest you go and talk to her.'

'And apologize,' said Flappy with a gulp. She did not like the thought of apologizing to Hedda.

'Yes. She doesn't need to know how long it's gone on for. Mr Harvey-Smith said it was just one kiss. You can say you got carried away with the tango and one thing led to another. Blame it on the drink and your medication.'

'What might the medication be for?' Flappy asked. Flappy

had never had to take medication of any kind. She was so very lucky to be in such good health.

'Depression,' said Persephone.

'Depression?'

'Yes, then she'll feel sorry for you.'

Flappy laughed grimly. She did not want Hedda to feel sorry for her, on any account. 'I hope we can keep it between us women,' she said.

'Exactly. I'll try and persuade George to keep it quiet, but I can't promise anything. I don't really know him. I'm not sure what he's going to do.'

'You like him, don't you?' said Flappy, turning and smiling at her in a maternal kind of way.

'I really do,' Persephone replied, smiling back.

'Young love,' said Flappy wistfully. 'It's a wonderful thing. Treasure it.'

'And by the way, I know you engineered my invitation to the party.'

'You do?'

'Yes, it was ingenious.'

Flappy laughed. It felt good to laugh when deep down she really wanted to cry. 'I have my ways,' she said. 'I'm happy it worked out. Even the best plans sometimes fail. George is handsome like his father. You make a fine couple. Did he like your dress?'

'He did,' said Persephone. 'Thank you, Flappy.'

'No, thank *you*, for rescuing me tonight.'

Persephone pulled the car up in front of the house and Flappy got out. 'Let's talk about this tomorrow when I've spoken to George. And try to get some sleep. I'll tell Mr Scott-Booth that I drove you home.'

Mr Scott-Booth, Flappy thought as she walked towards the front door of her beloved Darnley, so beautiful in the moonlight. *Mr Scott-Booth. How could I treat him with such little respect? After all he has given me over the years, the many years of our marriage. It's despicable. If any of my friends had behaved like that towards their husbands, I'd have shunned them. I'd have stood on my moral high ground, because it has always been so much higher than everyone else's, and lectured them about decency and restraint. But here am I, fallen from a great height, with my pride bruised and Charles's kisses turned to ash in my mouth, and I face losing everything. Darling Kenneth, my adorable Toad, can he ever forgive me?* Flappy began to cry. Big fat tears tumbled down her cheeks and plopped onto the marble floor as she walked slowly across the hall. She looked up at the portraits and her eyes lingered on Kenneth's. She hadn't looked at Kenneth's in a very long time. There he was in his yellow golfing clothes, sitting on a chair with his legs crossed, a golf club in his hand. His belly was round, his face shiny, his cheeks plump and pink and his smile wide and infectious, and Flappy's heart flooded with love. It poured into every nook and cranny like golden honey, and Flappy realized how much she had taken Kenneth for granted. It was a shocking admission. Only now, as she teetered on the point of losing him, did she realize how much she valued him.

She dragged herself up the sweeping staircase, indeed the staircase at Darnley was uniquely sweeping, and staggered into her bedroom. She fell onto her bed with a sob. *Oh, this is truly a dark night of the soul*, she thought, putting a pillow over her face and crying loudly. *I'm all alone!* she wailed. *My children are on the other side of the world, in fact, they couldn't be further away from me if they tried, and I'm going to lose my home, my precious Darnley, and my husband too. I will have nothing left but regret. And one cannot live with regret. It would be better if I threw myself out of the window. Yes! I should make my peace with God, whom I have treated almost as badly as I've treated Kenneth, then end it all.* She pushed herself off the mattress and went to the window. Outside, the round face of the moon smiled down at her, flooding the gardens, the magnificent gardens, in a soft, hoary light. How could the moon smile like that when Flappy was feeling so utterly desolate? She flung open the window and inhaled the sweet scent of damp earth and rotting leaves. The night was silent and still, guarding its secrets in the shadows that lingered in pools about the shrubbery and trees. Flappy raised her eyes to the stars. They twinkled in a velvety canopy above the lawn and she thought that, sure, the gardens at Compton Court were lovely, but *this* was something different altogether. This took one's breath away. This was heaven. And, if heaven was here at Darnley, there was no point jumping out of the window and leaving it.

Flappy heard the distinctive purr of Kenneth's Jaguar. Her stomach clenched, her heart contracted and she felt as if she might throw up. Hastily she wriggled out of her dress and pulled on her pyjamas. She dived under the duvet and turned off the light. She lay in silence for what felt like an eternity, listening out for the door but hearing only the thumping of her heart.

At length the front door opened and closed, and Kenneth's footsteps could be heard on the stairs. He was coming up fast. Flappy wondered whether he knew. Was he going to shout at her? Would she have to pack her bags now and take flight?

She held her breath.

Kenneth walked into the bedroom. Flappy squeezed her eyes shut. She felt his weight on the mattress as he sat down. Then she felt a hand stroking her hair. 'Darling, are you awake?'

Flappy pretended that she wasn't. Then she thought better of it and replied, weakly, 'Yes.'

'Are you all right? Persephone said she had to drive you home.'

'Oh, Kenneth,' she cried, sitting up and throwing her arms around him. 'I got drunk. I'm so ashamed! Did I make a fool of myself?'

'No, darling, you were marvellous. When did you learn to dance the tango like that? You were amazing! I was so proud.' Flappy felt sick with guilt. 'I hope you're not upset with me,' he added, squeezing her tightly.

'Upset with *you*? Why would I be upset with *you*?'

'Because I never came and congratulated you after your dance. I don't want you to think I was jealous of Charles. I'm not. I'm glad you had an opportunity to show everyone how beautifully you dance. But I should have been the first to congratulate you.'

Flappy kissed him on the cheek. 'You're sweet to think

of that. It would have been nice, of course, to have been congratulated by you. After all, your opinion is the only one that matters to me. But I didn't mind. In fact, I was a teeny bit tipsy, so I didn't notice. Then, I went into the garden to get some air and was overcome with nausea. Fortunately, Persephone was there and offered to drive me home. I didn't want to ruin your evening by asking *you*.'

'It was a wonderful party, wasn't it?' he said.

'The best party I've ever been to.'

'Jason Donovan, fancy that!'

'I know, they must be enormously rich,' said Flappy with a giggle.

Kenneth laughed too. He stood up. 'I won't keep you up. You must sleep. We can debrief over breakfast.'

'Darling, would you sleep in my bed tonight?' said Flappy, suddenly wanting to be held. 'I know it sounds silly, but I don't want to be alone.'

'If you like. I'll probably snore,' he warned her.

'I don't mind, in fact, I think I'll like the sound of my bed–pig tonight.'

'And I'll lie in in the morning,' he added.

'So will I,' she replied. 'We can lie in together.'

Kenneth changed into his pyjamas and brushed his teeth. Then he slid into bed beside his wife. She wriggled over and snuggled up against him. 'This is nice,' he said.

'Yes, it is,' she replied, relishing the feeling of being close. She wondered why she hadn't, for so many years, wanted to be close. She closed her eyes and tried not to think of George and what he might do.

'Night, darling,' said Kenneth and kissed her forehead.

'Night, Toad,' she replied. She hadn't called him Toad in a very long time. But it sounded right.

Chapter 16

Flappy awoke with a headache. That wasn't a surprise. However, the fact that Kenneth was pressed up against her in what people referred to as 'spooning' was. It was also a surprise to Flappy that she liked it. She looked at the clock on the bedside table. It was half past nine. She immediately thought of Persephone, waiting for her downstairs with news, and slid out of bed without waking him.

Hastily, she brushed her teeth and washed her face and slipped into her silk dressing gown and slippers. There was no point worrying about Persephone seeing her like this when the girl knew about her affair with Charles. After knocking back a couple of Panadols, she hurried downstairs.

Persephone was at her desk in the library. She looked bright-eyed and radiant for someone who had danced until dawn. 'What did he say?' Flappy asked, striding into the room and closing the door behind her.

Flappy could tell that it wasn't good news. She sat down with a terrible sinking feeling in her stomach.

'He's going to tell his mother,' said Persephone gravely and it clearly pained her to say it, because her bright eyes dimmed suddenly. 'He says it's happened before.'

Flappy swallowed. 'I see,' she said, sensing a horrible defeat.

'But he won't breathe a word to anyone else. As far as he knows it was a quick kiss in the walled garden and nothing more. He doesn't blame you. He says his father took advantage of you, as he has taken advantage of women before.'

Flappy nodded.

'I think you'd better drive over and see Hedda this morning.'

Flappy nodded again, a heaviness taking over from the sinking feeling, as if she were being filled with concrete. 'Yes, I suppose that is what I must do.'

'I'm sorry, Flappy. I tried to persuade him not to tell his mother.'

'I'm sure you did,' Flappy replied, but she couldn't smile. 'Thank you.'

'Would you like me to come with you? I can wait in the car.'

'No, that's okay. This is one battle I have to fight on my own.'

'Hedda might be more understanding than you think. If Charles has done it before.'

'She might, but on the whole, women are quick to blame other women.' She shrugged and her eyes drifted to the window. 'If it were me, I'm sure I'd blame *her*.'

'Can I make you a cup of coffee?' Persephone asked, feeling sorry for Flappy. She did not feel comfortable with

215

this new, crushed Flappy. She longed for the old, confident Flappy to return.

'Yes, come and keep me company. You can psyche me up before I go to the gallows.' Flappy laughed bitterly. 'Still, I can't complain. I've brought it all on myself.'

The two women went into the kitchen and Flappy sat down at the table. 'How was it with George last night?' she asked. 'Please tell me that you had a lovely evening. That will take the edge off my misery.'

Persephone smiled broadly. 'He kissed me,' she confessed.

Flappy's spirits lifted a little. 'Oh, I *am* pleased!' she exclaimed. 'I trust he's a good kisser. It's very important for the man to be a good kisser.'

'He is,' said Persephone, putting the coffee cup on the Nespresso machine. It made a whirring sound and then the smell of coffee wafted into the air. 'I think this is going to be serious,' she added. 'I have a good feeling about it.'

'So do I,' Flappy agreed. 'You know his great-uncle was a marquess? He's very grand.'

'No, I didn't,' said Persephone, who didn't care one way or the other.

'Oh yes, Hedda's money is old money. What does George do?'

'He's an architect and lives in London. In Shoreditch.'

Flappy didn't know any architects, nor did she know anyone who lived in Shoreditch, so it was impossible to box him. Flappy did like to box people according to their place in society. 'He's talented then,' she said. 'How lovely to have a talented boyfriend.'

216

'He's not my boyfriend,' said Persephone, but she was grinning.

'Yet,' said Flappy with emphasis. 'And don't go moving to Shoreditch, will you? Now I've got used to you, I don't think I can do without you.'

Persephone looked appalled. 'Of course I won't,' she said, bringing Flappy her cup of coffee. 'This is the best job I've ever had.'

'It's certainly rich and varied,' said Flappy with a shrug. 'But I won't underestimate the power of love.'

Flappy was still at the breakfast table when Kenneth appeared. He bent down and planted a kiss on her cheek. 'Good morning, darling,' he said.

'Good morning, Kenneth,' she replied, managing a small smile.

'How are you feeling?'

'Worse for wear. But it's totally my fault,' she said, watching him go to the bread bin and pop a piece in the toaster. 'Let me do that for you,' she added.

'No, you stay sitting down,' he insisted. 'I'll make breakfast this morning.'

Flappy was surprised. Kenneth hadn't made breakfast in a long time.

'What are your plans for today?' he asked.

Flappy dropped her gaze into her empty coffee cup. 'I'm going to whizz over to Hedda's to see if I can help with the clearing up.'

Kenneth looked baffled. Flappy was not one to volunteer to clear up. 'I thought we could have lunch at the golf club today.' He grinned. 'They do a delicious quiche.'

Flappy did not feel like being seen today, and yet, she didn't want to say no to Kenneth. 'I'd love that,' she said, hoping that, if he *did* find out about her and Charles, he'd take her enthusiasm to have lunch with him at the golf club into account.

At mid-morning Flappy drove down the winding lanes towards Compton Court. She had not called in advance to warn Hedda that she was coming. There was no point in doing that. For all she knew Hedda might refuse to see her. And Flappy *did* need to see her. She needed to plead her case. Indeed, she needed to put on the best performance of her life and apologize. However, apologizing did not come easily to Flappy because she was so rarely in the wrong. She wasn't even sure how to do it. She hoped that, when the moment came, she would instinctively know what to do.

Flappy did not notice the pretty colours as autumn breathed her cold breath onto the trees and hedges, curling their leaves and transforming them into reds and golds. She did not notice the cobalt skies, the fluffy white clouds or the gulls that circled above her. She thought only of her humiliation and her foolishness. Persephone had told her that Charles had done this before. That piece of information made Flappy feel sick. Flappy had *never* done this before, never *ever*. She'd thought that Charles hadn't either. She'd been under the impression that they were two people compelled to betray their spouses for the one and only time in their lives because they simply couldn't control their ardour for one another. How many times had Charles done this? she wondered. Had she been simply another conquest in a long line of conquests? She looked at herself in the rear-view mirror. 'You're a foolish old woman,' she told herself crossly. 'A *very* foolish old woman to fall for *that*.'

It was with a heavy heart that Flappy drove into the forecourt of Hedda's magnificent mansion. She walked up to the door. Her instincts were to climb straight back into the car and whizz off, but her head told her that that wasn't a sensible thing to do. She had come to apologize and apologize is what she would do, sincerely, regretfully and earnestly. With a trembling hand she rang the bell. She waited, barely daring to breathe, her heart racing so fast in her chest that she thought it might break out and fly away like a terrified bird. At last Johnson opened the door. 'Ah, Mrs Scott-Booth,' he said and smiled.

'Is Mrs Harvey-Smith available? I need to see her urgently.'

Johnson looked at her impassively. There was no indication from his expression that there might have been a massive row between husband and wife, or that Hedda might have locked herself in her bedroom and refused to come downstairs. He simply opened the door wider and invited her in. 'Please, come this way. Mrs Harvey-Smith is taking refuge in the garden.'

The mere mention of the word 'garden' caused Flappy's insides to turn over. But she followed Johnson as he led her at a frustratingly slow pace through the house and out to where the marquee was being dismantled by an army of shirtless men. Flappy did not want to see the marquee or any other evidence of the party, so she was relieved when Johnson led her away from the scenes of the night before and into the vegetable garden where Hedda was sitting on a bench in the sunshine, drinking a cup of tea. When she saw Flappy she smiled in surprise. Flappy was alarmed. Had George not yet told her?

'Darling Flappy, what are *you* doing here?' she asked.

'I need to talk to you,' said Flappy.

'How lovely. Johnson, will you bring Mrs Scott-Booth a cup of tea, no milk, with a slice of lemon. Come and sit down, Flappy. It's lovely here in the sunshine. I fear these are the final days of summer before it gets too cold to sit outside.'

'The party was wonderful,' said Flappy, sitting down next to Hedda.

Hedda grinned. 'It was, wasn't it?'

'I don't think I've ever been to such a beautifully organized event in all my life. Really, Hedda, you put anything I've ever done in the shade.'

'I don't believe that. From what I hear about your parties from Mary, they have a unique magic.'

'That's very sweet of her,' said Flappy, feeling incredibly small suddenly, and grateful for any compliment.

'So, what do you need to speak to me about?' Hedda asked. Her nonchalance told Flappy that she didn't know. Flappy was about to make something up, but nothing popped into her mind. Usually Flappy could count on something, but strangely this time, just when she needed it most, her mind was blank. There was nothing for it, she would have to tell Hedda about the kiss.

'Charles kissed me last night,' she said and her eyes filled with tears, because hurting Hedda was suddenly more dreadful than having to apologize. 'I'm so sorry, Hedda. I don't know what came over me. It must have been the drink, combined with my medication, you know, for depression . . . '

But Hedda put a hand on Flappy's arm and smiled kindly. 'Let me stop you right there,' she said. Flappy stopped and wiped her eyes, leaving her fingertips smudged with mascara. 'Firstly, I appreciate you coming to apologize. George told me this morning as he was very upset. You see, his father has done this before. I didn't expect you to come and see me. It just goes to show what a decent woman you are, Flappy.'

'No, I'm not,' said Flappy, needing now to tell her the whole truth so that there was nothing left to gnaw at her conscience. 'I'm awful. I'm the worst kind of woman there is. It wasn't just a kiss. Charles and I have been having an affair for the last three weeks.'

Hedda laughed. Flappy stopped crying. What on earth was there to laugh about?

'I know,' said Hedda. She stopped laughing and grew serious. 'How could I not know when Charles returned every evening smelling of tuberose?'

Flappy felt sick again. Hedda had often complimented her on her perfume.

'But I don't mind. You see, we have an arrangement. As long as he's discreet, he can sleep with whoever he likes.'

'You have an arrangement?' Flappy repeated in astonishment.

'Yes, in fact, I should be *thanking* you. The last thing I want to do is make love with my husband. I haven't wanted to for years. I shut the shop about a decade ago and told Charles he could get his oats elsewhere as long as he was discreet. The trouble is, he gets overexcited, and overconfident, and then gets caught. This is not the first time one of his children has caught him in flagrante delicto.'

'You knew all along and you didn't mind?' said Flappy, still trying to digest this extraordinary piece of information.

'Absolutely. The one thing about Charles is that he has very good taste. His choice of woman is always of the highest standard. I knew he'd go for you the moment I met you. In fact, I encouraged it. An hour's meditation every evening in your cottage was perfect. No one would know and there was little chance of him getting caught. You're happily married, so there wouldn't be any talk of divorce. You couldn't have been a better choice.'

'Oh, Hedda, I don't know what to say.' Which was quite an admission for Flappy because she *always* knew what to say.

Hedda patted her arm again. 'You don't need to say anything, but I'm afraid it must stop now. Charles has got his fingers burnt and he must be punished, otherwise, how's he ever going to learn to be discreet?'

'Oh, it's very much over. Very much,' said Flappy, overcome with relief.

'Please tell me you haven't confessed to Kenneth!' Hedda asked, putting a hand to her mouth at the thought that this might have gone further.

'No, I haven't and I won't. Kenneth doesn't need to know.'

'Quite,' Hedda agreed, dropping her shoulders with relief. 'Let's keep this between us girls, shall we?'

'Thank you, Hedda,' said Flappy, overcome with affection for Hedda.

'No, thank *you* for understanding, Flappy. There aren't many women who would understand, but you, Flappy, are not just any woman. You're unique and that's why I like you.' She turned her attention to Johnson, making his way towards them with a tray. 'Your tea,' she said. 'Now, let's not talk about Charles anymore. Let's talk about the tango. Where on earth did you learn to dance like that?'

When Flappy left Compton Court, she was buoyant with happiness. Her feet barely touched the gravel as she made her way to the car. All was forgiven. No one would ever mention it again. Kenneth was none the wiser and she and Charles were penitent. Flappy couldn't wait to tell Persephone. In fact, she decided, as she climbed into the car, that she would give the girl a rise in salary to thank her. That was the least she could do.

Flappy listened to Celine Dion's 'My Heart Will Go On' all the way back home, breaking into song during the chorus. She had suffered a terrible night of anxiety and remorse. It had really knocked her for six. She hoped she would never suffer another night like it. When she got home she went straight into the library to tell Persephone the good news.

'Hedda has forgiven me,' she told her.

223

Persephone was relieved. 'I'm so happy,' she said. 'That just goes to show what a big and generous-spirited person she is.'

'She's an aristocrat. That's what she is. They do things differently from the rest of us.'

'I think you're probably right. They're very open-minded,' said Persephone.

'I'm going on a detox,' Flappy announced. 'I'm not going to touch a drop of alcohol for a month. And I'm going to concentrate on my meditations and in cleansing the soul. If anyone's soul needs cleansing right now, it's mine.'

'Speaking of which, I believe I have found you a guru,' said Persephone.

'Really?' said Flappy.

'Yes, he just called while you were out.'

'Goodness, how wonderful. He's appeared just when I need him most. You do know what they say about gurus, don't you? That you don't find *them*, *they* find you.'

Persephone, who had most definitely found him herself, did not dampen Flappy's excitement by correcting her. 'He sounds very wise,' she said.

'What's his name?' Flappy asked.

'Murli,' said Persephone. 'He doesn't have a last name. He's just Murli.'

'And where does he live?'

'In town, so it's not too far for him to travel. He teaches yoga and meditation and is a life coach. But he doesn't advertise.'

'Of course he doesn't,' said Flappy approvingly.

'It was quite a challenge to find him.'

'*He* found *you*, remember?' said Flappy with a smile. 'Well, I could do with a life coach right now, couldn't I? When can I meet him?'

'I have taken the liberty of booking him in for tomorrow.'

'Tomorrow! How splendid. Once I've tried him out myself I'll let the girls know. They'll be so pleased to be included. I do think it's important, when one is as lucky as I am, to share one's luck.' Flappy made for the door. 'Just off for lunch at the golf club with Kenneth. To think that a day that started so badly could turn out so well!' And she grabbed her jacket from the hall and left the house with a skip.

Flappy drove through the black iron gates of the golf club. They were, surely, the grandest gates of any golf club in the country, she thought with satisfaction. Carved into a marble plaque on the wall, in large, unmissable gold letters, was the name Scott-Booth. If Flappy had been feeling a little down, which she wasn't, not anymore, the sight of her name displayed like that, so grandly, would have cheered her up. She didn't even have to stop at the barrier and give her name, for the official recognized her car at once and Flappy's face as she smiled and gave a royal wave and drove straight on through.

The clubhouse was a sprawling white building with a red-tiled roof and a wide veranda stretching the entire length of it. It was modern and functional, but lacked charm, which, had Flappy had a hand in the designing of it, would not have been the case. If there was one thing Flappy was good at, it was knowing what was good taste and what was not. The

Scott-Booth Golf Club was not. However, Flappy was in a generous mood, having been reprieved. She felt as if she had been walking to the gallows, only for the Queen to step in at the eleventh hour and declare a royal pardon. The slate had been wiped clean. It was as if her affair had never happened.

She parked her car in her own special place, marked clearly with the word 'RESERVED' in big letters above her name, and stepped out. It had been a while since she had been to the club. Usually, she would sweep her eagle eye over the pots of flowers either side of the front door and notice they needed watering, or pruning or dead-heading, and set about finding the person responsible. Today, she chose not to notice. She was not in the mood to be critical. She was in the mood to be kind.

She heard Kenneth's voice the moment she stepped into the reception hall. It was loud, with its own unique resonance, and happy. Kenneth was always happy. How *un*happy might he have been if things had turned out differently, she thought. What a near escape she'd had. But all's well that ends well, she mused, as she strode on towards the dining room. She pushed her sunglasses onto the top of her head and smiled at the members of staff in blue-and-green uniforms who acknowledged her deferentially. 'Good afternoon, Mrs Scott-Booth,' they said, and Flappy glanced at their badges and greeted them each by name.

Kenneth was at the bar with Charles, enjoying a beer. Flappy had not expected to see Charles and was a little taken aback. But she gathered herself, as only Flappy could, and smiled in her distinctively charming way. 'Charles,' she said.

'What a wonderful party you threw last night. I don't think Badley Compton will ever get over it.'

Charles's eyes were greener and brighter than usual and Flappy was surprised to find not a trace of remorse or contrition in them. 'Flappy,' he replied, planting a kiss on her cheek. 'I'm so happy you enjoyed yourself. It would not have been a party without you and your tango.'

'I didn't even know my wife could dance the tango,' said Kenneth with a chuckle. 'I should really learn a few steps so I can dance with her myself. It could be our showpiece.'

Flappy laughed. 'Darling, with all due respect, I think you should stick to golf!'

Kenneth laughed with her. Admittedly, dancing was not his thing. 'Darling, Charles is joining us for lunch. It's mayhem at Compton with all the clearing up.'

'How lovely,' said Flappy, but she did not catch Charles's eye. Something told her that, for him, nothing had changed.

The three of them went to the table and Kenneth ordered an expensive bottle of wine. Flappy ordered a cranberry juice, remembering her decision to give up alcohol for a month and wanting very much to stick to it. Flappy was not the sort of woman who made a resolution and then broke it.

At the end of lunch, when the waiter brought over their coffees and Flappy's mint tea (she was dismayed to see that it was not fresh but in a teabag), Kenneth excused himself and left the table to greet a friend. Flappy and Charles were left alone. There was an awkward silence, but Charles was keen to fill it. His gaze settled onto Flappy's face in a gentle caress and then he reached under the table and found her knee. 'I regret that I didn't sweep you up to one of the spare bedrooms and make love to you,' he said in a quiet voice.

Flappy was stunned. 'I've just been to see Hedda,' she told him, pushing his hand off her knee. 'It's over, Charles. Hedda knows.'

He laughed. 'Of course she knows and she doesn't mind,' he said. 'We have a deal.'

'I know all about your deal. But you've been caught. We agreed it has to stop.'

'She won't find out. We'll be careful.'

'I won't betray her, Charles. She's my friend.'

'Come on, Beauty! You can't ruin Beastie's fun.' He leaned closer and Flappy smelt the coffee on his breath, which, mixed with the wine, was not very appealing. 'Think of all the wicked things I'm going to do to you. No one else has ever brought you to such great heights of pleasure. Are you really going to give that up because of a friendship that is no more than a few weeks old?'

'Yes, Charles, I am. Hedda could have ruined my marriage and my reputation in this town, but out of the kindness of her heart she has decided not to.' Flappy looked at him with tenderness. 'What you and I had was wonderful and I wouldn't change any of it for the world. You are a wonderful lover. It is true. But we were careless and now we must pay the price. We can gaze at each other from afar, but we cannot touch. That's the way it has to be.'

Charles sat back in his chair and sighed. 'I won't give up, Beauty. I love you.'

'Oh, Charles . . .'

'I won't. I will give you time, that's all. Then I will return and sweep you off your feet again. You may think you are just another of my many conquests, but you are wrong. You are the greatest of all my conquests, and the last.'

Flappy was very pleased to hear that she was not only his greatest conquest but his last. She did not want to be arrogant – Flappy was aware of her faults and she did not believe that arrogance was one of them – but it did not surprise her in the slightest. After all, she was confident of her position at the top of the food chain. If she was certain of one thing, it was that she was a white tigress. However, as Kenneth made his way back to the table she was certain of something else, too. That she was happy with her Toad.

Chapter 17

Flappy waited impatiently in the hall. She was dressed all in white – a loose white shirt, white draw-string trousers, white plimsolls and a white shawl. In fact, she was a picture of innocence and serenity. It was just a shame that the ladies' tardiness disturbed the tranquillity of her mind, which up until this moment had been as calm as a limpid pool of water. Since meeting Murli, her guru – the guru sent to her by the universe, for it was true, one did not find a guru, the guru found one – meditation and yoga had done a great deal to put her back into balance and restore harmony to her life; she was herself again.

She looked at her watch and sniffed. If they didn't arrive soon she'd go without them.

The rumble of an engine and the scrunching of tyres on gravel broke the silence, and Flappy went outside. A chilly wind was blowing in off the sea now that autumn had staked her claim to the land and summer had well and truly retreated to flower on another continent far away. She folded her arms and looked disapproving. Mabel, who was

230

driving the car, gave a little wave, but Flappy did not wave back. They were late and if there was one thing Flappy abhorred, it was lateness.

The four women climbed out of the car. 'I'm so sorry, Flappy,' Mabel began nervously.

Esther followed behind her. 'We're only ten minutes late,' she said, glancing at her watch.

Madge hoped that Flappy would blame Mabel, seeing as she was driving the car. But Mabel reached Flappy and rolled her eyes. 'Madge couldn't find her yoga mat,' she explained.

'It's been so long since I've used it,' said Madge, hurrying over the gravel, the mat rolled up under her arm.

'We're all here now and I can't wait to meet the guru,' said Sally. 'What's he called?'

'Murli,' Flappy replied through tight lips. 'He's already there, probably mid-levitation by now. You know he's the real deal. Just as you would expect. A picture-perfect guru.' She swept her eyes over their yoga attire. Sally's, especially, was much too brightly coloured and brash. Flappy would make sure that she put Sally's mat behind hers so she wouldn't have to look at her. 'If one is going to have a guru, one might as well go the whole hog and have him long beard, long hair and all.'

'This is such fun!' gushed Mabel. 'I'm going to be very stiff. I can't even touch my toes.'

'I've never tried,' said Esther.

'I used to be able to put my ankles behind my ears,' added Madge.

Flappy put up a hand. 'That's not a pleasant thought, Madge. Shall we proceed?'

They followed Flappy through the gardens. A light mist lingered over the trees and shrubs, muting the reds and golds of the leaves and giving the place an almost Gothic beauty. Indeed, autumn at Darnley was really very beautiful and Flappy never missed an opportunity to remind herself of how incredibly lucky she was to live there – or to remind everyone else. 'I am so *so* lucky to be surrounded by such loveliness,' she said as she trod lightly down the path. 'Because to see nature's glory is to see the face of God.' She thought that sounded rather good and, since her infidelity, she was conscious of needing to make it up with God.

'Oh, it really *is* lovely,' Mabel agreed, admiring the swathes of Japanese anemones.

'I think that the gardens at Darnley are the loveliest in Badley Compton,' Madge added, knowing that *that* would earn her a few Brownie points.

It did indeed, for Flappy seemed to swell with pleasure. 'How kind of you, Madge. *I* think they're beautiful, but then of course I'm biased.'

'And the cottage is so dear,' said Sally as it came into view at the end of the path. 'Such a lovely secluded place for meditation.'

'Well, one is so frightfully busy,' said Flappy. 'One does need a little solitude every now and then, for one's soul.'

They all nodded in agreement, grateful that Flappy was herself once again.

Murli was indeed exactly as one would imagine a guru to

be. He had long white hair, a long white beard, rich brown skin, wise brown eyes and a large, sensitive nose. When he saw the women, he put the palms of his hands together and made a bow. The women followed suit, thrilled to be in the presence of a real guru who had come all the way from Rajasthan (albeit, some forty-six years ago).

'Welcome to my class,' he said, and his voice was exactly what a guru's voice should be, deep and soft and foreign.

Flappy was delighted to be showing off, not only the guru, of whom she was very proud because he was, to be sure, authentic, but the sanctuary, which was what she now called the sitting room, which Gerald had just completed. Incense filled the air, candles twinkled in their holders and the Buddha gazed upon them all with a wise and enlightened face.

They laid out their mats and the guru took them through the poses, explaining what each pose was for as he twisted his flexible body into all sorts of impossible positions. This one helped digestion, this one prevented headaches and this one aided concentration. Flappy, having done yoga every morning for the last thirty years, was able to hold each position with ease and obvious enjoyment. The others were like rusty old bicycles that hadn't been used in decades. Their wheels were stiff and their pedals creaked, but they were determined not to let Flappy down by complaining or giving up. By the end, Flappy had barely broken into a sweat while the others were as red in the face as runners after a marathon.

They settled onto their mats for the meditation. Flappy

arranged herself into the Lotus position, knowing that she and the guru were the only two in the room who could. Madge, who used to be able to put her ankles behind her ears, could no longer sit cross-legged, Sally could and did, while Mabel and Esther sat on chairs. The guru led them through a visualization which was very pleasant. Flappy stilled her mind and allowed it to follow the guru into a lush green forest, but then Charles popped out of the trees. She was determined not to think of him. It was over. Well and truly over. However, in spite of her efforts, her mind kept going back to him. After all, she'd been his best and last, and the fact that he'd said he'd never give up gave her a frisson of the old excitement that not so long ago had dominated her life. He still wanted her, a woman of her age! If Flappy abhorred one thing, it was smugness, yet she felt very smug about that.

At the end of the meditation, when the guru gently brought them back to the present, they were flushed in the face and unusually peaceful. They hadn't quite reached Nirvana, that was reserved for those like Flappy who were very advanced, but they had, nonetheless, reached some-where surprisingly pleasant.

'We will finish with an "Om",' said the guru. 'It is a simple word but it has a very complex meaning. The whole universe resonates with the vibration of "Om". So when we chant, we connect with the deep, eternal sound of the universe, yes? We say "Om", but we chant "Aum". Understood? Let's try.'

He closed his eyes, placed his hands in the prayer position, and began to chant. The women chanted with him. The sound started in their chests, rose up their windpipes and escaped through their mouths. Esther tried not to laugh; Madge was overcome with nostalgia for the retreat she'd been to many years ago in India; Mabel concentrated very hard because she wanted to be like Flappy; and Sally was distracted by a new story that was coming into her mind from nowhere about a married woman who meets her lover in a cottage like this one, under the guise of practising yoga.

Flappy lost her sense of self in the vibration. She found that she was spiralling down somewhere deep inside herself, very far away. It was a blissful feeling to be so relaxed and so disconnected from one's life. She could have stayed there all evening, but the guru had to go. He had another client to see and Flappy was called back.

'Where did you go?' asked Mabel, when the guru had left and Flappy had opened her eyes, looking dazed and strangely peaceful.

Flappy sighed and gave her a beatific smile. 'Into my soul, Mabel,' she said.

'What was it like?' asked Madge.

'Still,' she replied. 'Isn't it wonderful that one's soul is so still, when one's mind is so terribly busy!' She stood up and stretched. 'How was that, ladies?' She scrutinized them with a sharp and critical gaze.

'I adored it,' gushed Mabel.

'Wonderful,' said Madge.

Esther wasn't convinced. 'I'm afraid meditation is not for me,' she said.

235

'You have to keep at it,' said Flappy. 'It's something you get better at the more you do. You're not giving up, Esther. Things that are worth having do not come without effort. Don't think that I reached such depths the first time I did it. It's taken many times to get this good.'

'But we don't have your focus,' said Sally.

Flappy knew this was true, but she didn't want to make her friends feel inadequate. If there was one thing Flappy was good at, it was making other people feel good about themselves. 'Yes, you do,' she said firmly. 'You all have the potential to be the best versions of yourselves possible and it starts here, with me.' She put out her hand. 'Who's going to join me on the road to Enlightenment?'

Mabel was the first to put her hand on top of Flappy's. 'Me,' she said.

'Me,' said Madge, putting hers on top of Mabel's.

'All right,' agreed Sally. 'Me too.'

'Come on, Esther,' encouraged Flappy with a smile. 'I might be a little further along the path than you, but you never know, with effort and dedication you might catch up.'

'Okay,' said Esther, although she thought the whole thing a complete waste of time. Esther placed her rough old palm on the top of the pile. 'I'm in,' she said with a grin. 'And if I don't reach Nirvana, Flappy, I want my money back.'

And Flappy laughed for she was paying for the guru, or rather Kenneth was. Darling Kenneth. She was so *so* lucky to have Kenneth.

On the second Sunday in November, Flappy opened her curtains to see the gardens crystallized with frost. She caught her breath. The beauty of it was arresting. Dawn was but a faint golden light on the horizon, breaking through the night's sky like the distant glow of a farrier's forge. The lawn and the bushes and trees were silver-grey and still, like a magical world where fawns are half human and half beast and children appear out of wardrobes with their faces full of wonder. Flappy was filled with joy, because that's what beauty did to her, it made her feel buoyant, as if the lightness in her heart could literally lift her off her feet and send her flying over the gardens like an owl. She smiled and inhaled through her nose. She was happy and grateful, and aware of all her blessings. Indeed, Flappy had more blessings than she could count. But the greatest blessing of all was in her bed.

Kenneth, who was now invited to join her every Saturday night, lay sleeping in the semi-dark. He snored and grunted and made all sorts of revolting noises, but Flappy considered that her penance for her transgression. She not only put up with it, she welcomed it, for every snore and grunt reminded her of her sin and inspired her to become a better person. That said, she did not go as far as allowing him to make love to her. That would be one step too far and Kenneth might suspect something. It was very important that he didn't. Besides, now she was further along the path of Enlightenment the beast within had been cast back into the shadows and her carnal desires had been extinguished. She was more spirit than matter, and getting increasingly spiritual by the day.

Quietly she left the bedroom and went down to practise yoga. She did not swim naked in the pool. That urge had been relegated to the shadows with the beast, and she did not dance to pop music. She practised yoga in front of the mirror and tried not to admire her beautiful figure because that would be succumbing to pride.

After yoga she went to the kitchen to help herself to breakfast. The newspapers had been delivered and, as usual, she secretly read the *Mail on Sunday* while Kenneth slept on, leaving the *Sunday Telegraph* by his place for when he came down and joined her. Flappy devoured the gossip in the paper, flicked through *You Magazine* and sipped her tea. By the time Kenneth appeared, the *Mail* was nowhere to be seen and Flappy was ready by the coffee machine with a wide smile and a kind word, the perfect wife in the perfect kitchen in the perfect life, at Darnley.

Flappy got ready for church. She wore an elegant long skirt over boots, a black cashmere sweater and three rows of pearls at her throat with matching pearl earrings. She admired herself in the mirror, certain that she lived up to the expectations of the good people of Badley Compton, whom she would see at church. She did not want to disappoint. After all, Mabel needed an example to copy and the other women needed someone to admire. It was an arduous task, being an arbiter of style, but someone had to do it and Flappy was aware that she was the only person in Badley Compton who qualified. As she climbed into Kenneth's Jaguar she was secure in the knowledge that her position as queen of Badley Compton was unchallenged.

Kenneth parked the car outside the church and they walked slowly up the path, arm in arm, the last to arrive, as was tradition. They passed through the big doors and breathed in the familiar smell of candle wax, warm bodies and perfume, mingled with the particular scent of this ancient place of worship. Everything was as it should be, Flappy thought as she made her way down the aisle at a stately pace, smiling graciously at all her friends and acquaintances who turned their heads to admire her. She was happy to see, at the front, in the row behind Hedda and Charles, Persephone and George, who had been inseparable since the party – Hedda's event was now referred to simply as that and Flappy was not in the least jealous. She'd just make sure that she gave a bigger one next year.

Flappy smiled at the vicar, who was looking a little uneasy, and turned to the left. To her horror, there, sitting in her and Kenneth's seats, was a couple she had never seen before. She stopped and stared, and a look of total bewilderment and affront darkened her face. The couple didn't even look at her, they were busy with their noses in their prayer books. There was no apology, no getting up and moving somewhere else, no hint of awareness that they had, in front of the entire community, made a terrible faux pas. In one hasty glance, Flappy, with her incisive eye, took in the woman. She must have been in her thirties, with rich brown hair, smooth olive skin, high cheekbones, a wide and beautiful face – yes, it must be acknowledged that she was, indeed, very beautiful – and a pretty, straight nose. She was elegant, too, in a belted blue coat with a fur lapel.

Flappy coughed. The woman looked up. Flappy noticed that her eyes were beautiful too. Pale sage-green in colour and surrounded by thick black lashes of an indecent length. The woman smiled innocently. Flappy's indignation deepened. Kenneth put a hand on her arm and encouraged her to come away. If it hadn't been for Flappy's innate graciousness and her desire to be polite at all times – she was, after all, quite advanced up the path of Enlightenment – she would have told the couple to move. But she didn't. She allowed her husband to lead her away. Hedda and Charles squeezed up to allow them to sit in their row and Flappy sat down beside Hedda.

'How dare they!' Hedda hissed to Flappy under her breath.

'Who *are* they?' Flappy hissed back.

'I don't know, but I fear they are new in Badley Compton.'

'You mean they've *moved* here?' Flappy was appalled. 'They're here to stay?'

'I believe so. They spent a long time talking to the vicar.'

'Did they, indeed?'

'They need to be told,' whispered Hedda. 'They can't swan in here as if they own the place and sit in the front row! Who do they think they are?'

'You're right, they need to be told,' Flappy agreed.

'There's a pecking order in this town and they can't jump straight to the top of it.'

'You're so right.'

'But we must do it subtly.'

'Absolutely. You're so right, Hedda.' If there was one thing Flappy was good at, it was knowing when to be subtle.

'Come for tea this afternoon so we can discuss it.'

'I will. It's a matter of some urgency.'

'I'd say it most certainly is.'

'How dare they.'

'How dare they, indeed.'

Acknowledgements

I had such fun writing about Flappy Scott-Booth in my novel *The Temptation of Gracie* that I was inspired to give her a book of her own. In the wake of publication, I received so many emails about her, for she seemed to give my readers a lot of pleasure even though she's a very small character, that I itched to give her a bigger role and really expand the character. However, this wasn't possible because I just didn't have the time to write my usual annual novel, which takes at least six months, the *Royal Rabbits* children's series, which I write with my husband, Sebag, and a Flappy book. Still, I longed to write it, not least because I was keen to try something different and write a comedy for a change. It would be nice not to make people cry for once! It was only when the country was sent into Lockdown because of the dreaded Covid-19 that I decided, rather than spend the time feeling anxious, I might as well channel my energy into something positive and creative. Hence *Flappy Entertains* was finally written.

I have dedicated this book to five of my best girlfriends. We're a book club, a travel club, a lunch and dinner club but above all a group of friends who are in for the long haul, through both good times and bad. They keep me entertained. They keep me sane. But above all I know that when the chips are down, which they inevitably are sometimes, they're there to restore my spirit with compassion, understanding and laughter. Thank you, Tiff Beilby, Lisa Carter, Brigitte Dowsett, Wendy Knatchbull and Clare Rutherford.

I also want to thank my agent, Sheila Crowley, and my editor, Suzanne Baboneau, for being so enthusiastic about this new direction I'm taking. They embraced Flappy immediately and were as excited as I am about embarking on a comedy series. In the face of uncertainty and growing anxiety, we really do need to laugh!

I am also grateful to my film agent, Luke Speed, and to all those at Curtis Brown who work on my behalf: Alice Lutyens, Enrichetta Frezzato, Katie McGowan, Claire Nozierers and Callum Mollison. A huge thank you to Ian Chapman, my boss at Simon & Schuster, and his brilliant team who work so diligently and sensitively on my manuscripts: Sara-Jade Virtue, Gill Richardson, Dominic Brendon, Polly Osborn, Rich Vlietstra and Alice Rodgers.

I also thank my daughter Lily, my sister-in-law Sarah and my mother Patty Palmer-Tomkinson for reading the first draft and getting Flappy's point. It was a new direction for me and they gave me the encouragement I needed to keep at it. Creating a character who is at once pretty dreadful but loveable is quite a challenge!

Thank you to the rest of my family for making Lockdown the very special time it was: Sasha Sebag-Montefiore, Simon

Sebag-Montefiore, Charlie Palmer-Tomkinson, James Palmer-Tomkinson, Honor Palmer-Tomkinson, India Palmer-Tomkinson, Sam Palmer-Tomkinson, Wilf Palmer-Tomkinson and Naomi Dawson.

I hope this will be a series of many Flappy adventures. I haven't had so much fun writing in a long time! And I think Flappy deserves a series. She'd pretend she was honoured and perhaps a teeny bit embarrassed to be the focus of so much attention, and she'd tell everyone that she's so *so* lucky to be the subject of a novel, but in reality, she'd consider it her due. After all, it must be acknowledged, she is awfully fascinating!

Don't miss the brand-new novel by *Sunday Times* bestselling author Santa Montefiore ...

Faced with losing everything, all that matters is ...

HERE *and* NOW

Marigold has spent her life taking care of those around her, juggling family life with the running of the local shop, and being an all-round leader in her quiet yet welcoming community. When she finds herself forgetting things, everyone quickly puts it down to her age. But something about Marigold isn't quite right, and it's becoming harder for people to ignore.

As Marigold's condition worsens, for the first time in their lives her family must find ways to care for the woman who has always cared for them. Desperate to show their support, the local community come together to celebrate Marigold, and to show her that losing your memories doesn't matter, when there are people who will remember them for you ...

Evocative, emotional and full of life, *Here and Now* is the most moving book you'll read this year – from *Sunday Times* bestselling author Santa Montefiore.

AVAILABLE NOW IN PRINT AND EBOOK

**SIMON &
SCHUSTER**

Look out for the *Sunday Times* bestseller from
Santa Montefiore ...

The SECRET
HOURS

*'Let the wind take me and the soft rain settle me into the
Irish soil from where I came. And may my sins be forgiven ...'*

Arethusa Clayton has always been formidable, used to getting her
own way. On her death, she leaves unexpected instructions. Instead
of being buried in America, on the wealthy East Coast where she
and her late husband raised their two children, Arethusa has decreed
that her ashes be scattered in a remote corner of Ireland, on the
hills overlooking the sea.

All Arethusa ever told Faye was that she grew up in a poor farming
family and left Ireland, alone, to start a new life in America as did so
many in those times of hardship and famine. But who were her
family in Ireland and where are they now? What was the real reason
that she turned away from them? And who is the mysterious
benefactor of a significant share of Arethusa's estate?

AVAILABLE NOW IN PRINT AND EBOOK

**SIMON &
SCHUSTER**

booksandthecity.co.uk
the home of female fiction

| NEWS & EVENTS | BOOKS | FEATURES | COMPETITIONS |

Follow us online to be the first to hear from
your favourite authors

bc

booksandthecity.co.uk

@TeamBATC

Join our mailing list for the latest news, events and
exclusive competitions

Sign up at
booksandthecity.co.uk